MURDER AT HIGH TIDE

A ROSA REED MYSTERY

LEE STRAUSS
NORM STRAUSS

la plume PRESS

Library and Archives Canada Cataloguing in Publication Title: Murder at High Tide : a 1950s cozy historical mystery / Lee Strauss. Names: Strauss, Lee (Novelist), author. Description: Series statement: A Rosa Reed mystery ; 1 Identifiers: Canadiana (print) 20200175505 | Canadiana (ebook) 20200175513 | ISBN 9781774090862 (hardcover) | ISBN 9781774090886 (softcover) | ISBN 9781774090879 (IngramSpark softcover) | ISBN 9781774090848 (EPUB) | ISBN 9781774090855 (Kindle) Classification: LCC PS8637.T739 M84 2020 | DDC C813/.6—dc23

ROSA REED MYSTERIES
IN ORDER

Murder at High Tide
Murder on the Boardwalk
Murder at the Bomb Shelter
Murder on Location
Murder and Rock 'n' Roll
Murder at the Races
Murder at the Dude Ranch

SUMMARY

Murder's all wet!

It's 1956 and WPC (Woman Police Constable) Rosa Reed has left her groom at the altar in London. Time spent with her American cousins in Santa Bonita, California is exactly what she needs to get back on her feet, though the last thing she expected was to get entangled in another murder case!

If you love early rock & roll, poodle skirts, clever who-dun-its, a charming cat and an even more charming detective, you're going to love this new series!

The Rosa Reed Mystery series is a spin-off of the acclaimed Ginger Gold Mystery series.

This book has been edited and proofed, but typos are like little gremlins that like to sneak in when we're not looking. If you spot a typo, please report it to: **admin@leestraussbooks.com**

Rosa & Miguel's Wartime Romance is a BONUS short story exclusively for Lee's newsletter subscribers.

Subscribe Now!

1

*H*ugging was a very "un-English" thing to do.

Rosa Reed, rather British through and through, had yet to acclimatize to the exuberance of the American branch of her family and had endured more hugs in the few days she'd been in Santa Bonita, California than she'd had for most of her life growing up in Great Britain, the war years excepted. Now that she and her cousin Gloria had arrived at her Aunt Louisa's charity event on the beach, Rosa braced herself for even more.

Drinks and cigarettes in hand, a crowd of people milled about, standing or sitting at round tables covered in white linen. Catering staff, all dressed in white, were busy fussing with the food.

"I feel overdressed," Rosa remarked to her younger cousin Gloria Forrester. Red ribbons adorned Rosa's white dress that was sprinkled with black polka dots. Short chestnut-colored waves were crowned with a white straw sun hat trimmed with matching red ribbon.

"You're a Forrester," Gloria said. With dark hair curled tightly around her ears, and dark lipstick on a bright white smile, Gloria spun to show off the fancy baby-blue crinoline skirt of her swing dress. "You're supposed to overdress."

Rosa grinned. Gloria Forrester was seven years Rosa's junior and often seemed younger than her twenty-one years.

"And that dress," Gloria continued, motioning a white-gloved hand toward Rosa, "is fabulous!"

"Another perk of having a mother who owns a prestigious Regent Street dress shop," Rosa said.

"I love Feathers & Flair! Shopping there was the highlight of my trip." Gloria's eyes, briefly wide with wonder, now darkened in shock. Her gloved hand flew to her mouth. "I'm sorry. I wasn't thinking."

"It's fine, Gloria," Rosa said, forcing her voice to sound light. "Ancient history."

If one considered a month ancient. Perhaps in California, but not in England. A month was like a breath, and Rosa still felt the sting and humiliation of what had, in front of many witnesses including the members of the Forrester family, been a failed attempt down the aisle.

Gloria removed her sandals, hooked the straps over one hand, and motioned for Rosa to do the same. Rosa grinned at the sight of the two of them, dressed for a party yet barefoot on the beach. She was glad Gloria had reminded her not to wear stockings.

Gloria linked her arm with Rosa's and pulled her down the beach—those bad memories left behind them, for now.

"There's Mom." Gloria pointed to a slim, attractive woman in her early fifties who held a martini in one hand.

Louisa Forrester, the half-sister to Rosa's mother Ginger Reed, saw the young ladies approaching and broke into a smile. Handing her drink to one of her companions, Louisa gracefully stepped toward them, the hem of her stunning black evening dress flirting with the sand.

"Girls! There you are!" Aunt Louisa spread her arms wide apart.

Rosa hesitated, then briefly succumbed to the squeezing, despite the public setting.

With one hand still on Rosa's shoulder, her aunt stepped back and appraised her with a long glance. "You do look pale, though, Rosa. We need to get you in the sun."

Rosa grimaced inwardly. Affection mixed with criticism was Aunt Louisa's way. Besides, she'd spent plenty of time in the sun, though she did concede to being a shade dweller. Her fair skin burned easily.

At least Aunt Louisa had stopped commenting on her accent. She was determined to, in her words, "make an American out of you again".

"Gloria probably didn't fill you in on the purpose of this event," Aunt Louisa started. "It's a fundraiser for one of my charities. I serve on several boards. This one is for the California Polio Research Foundation. You've heard of the March of Dimes that President Roosevelt instituted in the thirties? There's a loose association with that."

Aunt Louisa pointed to a large banner that hung over the buffet tables with the CPRF—California Polio Research Foundation—logo emblazoned on it. "I want you to meet some people who help with the charity." She turned back to the lady still holding her martini. "This is Florence Adams, or 'Flo' as we like to call her. She was invaluable to me in planning this whole evening."

Florence Adams, in a red crushed-satin party dress, handed the martini back to Aunt Louisa. Flicking her blonde ponytail over her shoulder, Flo smiled to reveal straight white teeth and a wide, expressive mouth. An attractive woman with tanned skin that crinkled slightly around the corners of her blue eyes, regarded Rosa.

"Hello, hello," she said rather loudly. Her arms opened wide, and Rosa accepted the unsolicited hug. Miss Adams' speech had a slight slur, and the smell of brandy on her breath was strong. "Your aunt has told me all about you. I hope—I hope your stay in Santa Bonita goes well. Are you here for very long?"

That was a question Rosa didn't know how to answer. Her nuptials disaster had made Rosa desperate to escape London. She'd taken a leave of absence of an undetermined length from her job with the Metropolitan Police and booked a one-way flight.

Lifting a drink from a passing cocktail tray, Gloria handed Rosa the delicate crystal glass and answered for her. "She is going to stay for as long as she likes." She launched into a faux London accent. "This poor copper needs a break, and I intend to make her enjoy every minute of it."

Aunt Louisa interrupted two people seated at a nearby table who seemed deep in conversation. She put her hand on one of the young men, his khaki shorts exposing steel and leather leg braces.

"Please excuse me," she said. "I'd like you to meet my niece. Rosa, this is Rod Jeffers. Rosa just arrived from London."

"Great to meet you," the young man said, nodding his head.

Aunt Louisa went on. "Rod works with us in public relations and is excellent with the press and any aspects of promoting our charity."

Continuing her introductions, Rosa's aunt motioned to the man Mr. Jeffers had been engaging with. "This is Raul Mendez, the treasurer of our little organization. But don't think him a bore. He's also a great bassist and is playing in the band we have here tonight."

The young man smiled thinly as he stood and briefly took Rosa's hand. "Welcome to Santa Bonita. Now, if you'll excuse me, I'd like to get some food, ya know, before the band's finished its break." Mr. Mendez shuffled through the sand toward the makeshift stage in the distance.

Rosa continued to smile as she was put on display and introduced to her aunt's many friends and acquaintances. She just hoped she could keep all the names straight, should she meet these people again after tonight.

Aunt Louisa waved an arm and shouted, "Shirley! Shirley!" She was loud enough that Rosa thought, perhaps, Florence Adams wasn't the only one to have had a bit too much to drink. However, Rosa knew her aunt well enough to know that she would never get to a point where she was out of control. Control was far too important to her.

Shirley, a middle-aged woman with a thick waistline and round cheeks, turned at the sound of her name, and if Rosa's instincts were right, forced a smile she didn't feel.

"Rosa, this is Mrs. Shirley Philpott, Flo's cousin and the wife of our chief medical examiner, Dr. Melvin Philpott." Shirley nodded at Rosa. "Shirley, this is my niece, Rosa Reed, from England. You'll get a kick out of her accent."

Mrs. Philpott laughed at that. "Now, you must say something!"

"How do you do?" Rosa said politely.

"Oh, you're right, Mrs. Forrester. She's adorable. Come now, give me a hug!"

"Oh," Rosa muttered as Mrs. Philpott, soft and doughy, almost squeezed the wind out of her.

Mrs. Philpott released her but held her shoulders with two strong hands. "Say something else."

"I find your accent charming as well."

"Oh," Mrs. Philpott laughed. "Just like the Queen."

Being a novelty conversation starter for her American family was becoming the norm for Rosa. If she wanted, she could revert to the American accent she'd picked up during her stay at the Forrester mansion during the war years. Having spent her impressionable teens under Aunt Louisa's tutelage had left a deep and lasting mark. She just didn't know if she wanted to. Her London heritage had a deep meaning for her.

An older, jovial man wearing dark-rimmed spectacles and a cream-colored three-piece suit joined them, and it was Mrs. Philpott's turn to make introductions. "Honey, this is Louisa's niece, Rosa. She has the most adorable accent. This is my husband, Dr. Philpott."

Only in California could one get away with wearing a formal suit while barefooted, Rosa mused.

He extended his hand. "Your aunt tells me you are a police officer! Well then, I'm sure you are very familiar with us pathologist types." He chuckled as he took a puff from a cigarette.

"Yes, I am," Rosa replied. "In fact, vampires and medical examiners are my specialties." She pronounced it "speshee-al-i-ties" and immediately realized how British she sounded at that moment. "One can usually find both hovering over someone newly cold," she quipped.

"Ha! I like this girl!" Melvin Philpott chuckled and raised his glass. "To one of London's finest." They all raised a glass and took a sip, and Rosa couldn't help but feel a tad embarrassed.

The group continued chattering, and Rosa soon wanted to be alone, even if to simply walk the beach and watch the sunset. With her shoes in hand, she placed her empty glass on the buffet table and wandered away from the crowd. Soon, all she could hear was the distant music from the band and the crashing of the surf. She sat down on a large piece of driftwood and released a slow breath. Had it only been five days since her mum and dad had taken her to the airport and waved her off?

The voices of two women coming from the beach behind her interrupted her thoughts. Turning to the sound, Rosa saw the two were immersed in an intense argument. In the fading light, Rosa could just make out the forms of Shirley Philpott and Florence Adams, seemingly too engaged in verbal sparring to notice her.

With the crash of the waves and the squawking of the seagulls flying overhead, Rosa couldn't make out what was being said. Mrs. Philpott pointed at Miss Adams, who immediately slapped her cousin's finger away. Shirley Philpott tried to placate the younger woman, but Miss Adams was having none of it.

Florence Adams shouted at the top of her lungs, "My glass is empty, and I know where to get some more of the good stuff!" She then stormed off in the opposite direction of the party. Shirley Philpott threw her hands up in the air one last time before she lumbered back to the gathering.

Rosa wished she hadn't heard or seen the family

spat and determined to clear her mind of it. Rising to her feet, she walked into the water and enjoyed the feel of the warm, gentle surf on her toes. She continued along the beach as it curved inward until the party was no longer in her line of sight, and the music had faded away.

Just up ahead, Rosa saw Flo Adams walking toward a bank of houses, each with porch lights illuminating the beach. Near a beach access stairway, Miss Adams met up with a man who wore khaki pants and a loose-fitting Hawaiian shirt. Even from this distance, Rosa could see he was fit and good-looking.

Determined to ignore the couple, Rosa continued her walk, but when she saw the man grab Florence by the arm, her police instincts kicked in, and she stopped.

Great, she thought. Just what she didn't need in her life—more drama. How far did she have to travel to find peace?

After a moment, the man released Miss Adams' wrist, but when she turned to leave, the man stepped in front of her. It disturbed Rosa when the man cupped the back of Florence's head as if he intended to force a kiss.

Rosa took a step toward the couple, but then Florence swiped away the man's hand and stormed off. Rosa stopped in her tracks and let out a breath of relief.

She pivoted back toward the party before Aunt Louisa decided to send out a search party for her.

The smooth voice of the lead singer of the band grew louder as Rosa drew closer, and she recognized Frank Sinatra's "South of the Border". Despite all her previous efforts, her mind betrayed her by flying to the memory of an American serviceman of Mexican descent who'd been stationed in Santa Bonita during the war.

Private Miguel Belmonte had been Rosa's first love. The first time he'd turned his smile on her, deep dimples in his cheeks, she'd melted like a plate of butter left in the hot sun. Rosa often wondered if the stolen moments she and Miguel had shared during those four wonderfully agonizing months so long ago had ruined her for anyone else. Was this why she couldn't go through with marrying Winston?

The emotions rushed hotly through her as if the "shame" she'd brought on the Forrester family had happened only yesterday. Aunt Louisa had been livid, a living volcano, spewing lava of unkind words. Rosa had not only fallen for a poor man, but she'd also dared to love a Mexican. Mostly service people, especially in 1945, the Mexicans worked in mansions like Aunt Louisa's and came in through the back door. This Belmonte boy would keep Rosa in poverty. Would ruin the family name. Did Rosa want that?

But seventeen-year-old Rosa hadn't had much of a say. As soon as the war ended, Aunt Louisa booked her a ticket back to London, where her parents had eagerly waited, unaware of their only daughter's broken heart.

Funny how returning to the place of one's childhood stirred up so many emotional memories.

She walked closer to the band's stage to join a handful of onlookers. The song was winding down to its end. The singer, dressed in khaki pants and a short-sleeve cotton shirt, hit the last note with a flourish and turned to smile at the crowd as they applauded. His gaze fell on Rosa, his copper-brown eyes registering surprise.

Miguel Belmonte.

Their eyes locked and everything around them—the people, the noise, Aunt Louisa's throaty laughter—faded away, with only the sound of Rosa's heart pounding in her ears like an angry thundercloud.

And then a woman's shrill scream filled the air.

2

*R*osa instantly sprinted towards the scream, every police reflex on full alert. So focused on the urgency of the moment, she failed to notice how her crinoline slip chafed her thighs, or how the sand stuck to her bare calves. On the edge of the beach where light from the party still extended, Rosa approached a body on its back, half covered by the surf.

The screamer, a distressed young lady who seemed to be on the verge of fainting found her tongue. "Oh my God. I think she's dead!"

Gloria, who appeared acquainted with the lady, ran over to support her. "Vanessa! Are you all right?"

Rosa's gaze moved from her cousin and the poor girl who'd stumbled over the tragic scene to the body before them, a female with strands of wet blonde hair obscuring her face was soaked from the latest splash of waves. Rosa was quite sure the woman was dead but squatted low to put two fingers to the neck. She frowned. No pulse.

Rosa recognized the dress, now drenched and marred with bits of seaweed. She didn't have to see the face to know who it was.

A crowd quickly gathered, and exclamations of surprise and distress could be heard as more people arrived. Rosa heard cries of "Oh my God," "Is she dead," and "Who is she?" circulate through the crowd.

As she turned the body onto its side, Rosa hoped to clear any water from the mouth, but none dribbled out. Failing to find any sign of life, she let the body fall back.

"Okay, everyone. Back away."

Rosa instantly recognized the voice and glanced up at Miguel before standing and backing away as instructed. His shock at seeing her was still evident on his face. This time, he spoke loudly for the crowd's benefit. "I'm a police officer. Please step back."

Rosa blinked. *A police officer?*

Dr. Melvin Philpott, who had just broken into the circle and was breathing hard, said, "Oh my."

Squatting, Dr. Philpott also checked the pulse. His face was grim. He finally turned to Miguel and slowly shook his head.

Rosa scanned the crowd. Experience told her that

even if a death initially appeared to be accidental, it could just as well be a homicide. If it was, it was also likely that the killer was still in the area and might even be part of this charity fundraiser event. It was possible, if not probable, that he or she was in this very crowd, looking on.

Without drawing attention to herself, Rosa took a few steps back into the crowd to observe people's reactions. The art of reading facial expressions and body language was something that her mother, a renowned London private investigator, had taught her.

A hush had descended on the stunned onlookers. Horror-struck people covered their mouths while others stood on tiptoes for a better view. A woman in the back mewed softly.

Rosa startled at the sight of her cousin Clarence, who made a right scene earlier about not attending another one of his mother's events. Looking rather out of place on the beach, he wore belted shorts, and shoes with argyle socks pulled to the knee. He watched her intently with a strange, bemused look on his face. *When had he arrived?*

Rod Jeffers stood by his table in the distance leaning on an arm crutch. Next to him, Raul Mendez poked the sand with a stick while idly observing people's reactions to the body. Shirley Philpott was nowhere to be seen.

Rosa also noticed a man standing in the surf just in the shadow beyond the reach of the lights. It was hard to tell, but it looked like the man she had seen earlier trying to steal a kiss from Florence Adams. The man seemed to notice Rosa looking at him and quickly backed into the darkness. Rosa automatically catalogued these observations in her mind and looked at her watch to check the exact time. Apparently, the detective in her refused to go off duty.

In a loud voice, Miguel said, "Please, everyone remain calm. Can someone please run to the nearest phone and call an ambulance and the police department?"

Pushing his glasses up on his nose, Raul Mendez volunteered, turned, and jogged toward the parking lot and the nearest homes.

"Did anyone see what happened?" Miguel addressed the crowd. "Maybe up on the pier?" He scanned the group, but a sense of corporate dread fell, and no one spoke up.

"The tide is coming in," Mr. Philpott said in a voice that was calm but firm. "We need to move her."

Miguel nodded. "Okay, I need everyone to back away, but please stay on the beach until the police arrive. Until then, let's let Dr. Philpott do his job."

The crowd slowly dispersed with people wandering back to the safety of the stage and food area where the lights illuminated the beach. Most were speaking quietly and hugging each other. Speaking to the distraught Vanessa in soft tones, Gloria guided her away from the scene.

As Rosa approached, Aunt Louisa stood to the side, her mouth agape. "I can't believe this is happening! All the planning, all the invitations, the food . . ." She threw her hands up in the air, her eyes hard with anger. "Is it really Florence?"

Rosa nodded. "I'm afraid so."

Shirley Philpott's voice reached Rosa before the boisterous woman came into view. "What's going on?" She bounded through the sand like a happy hippopotamus. "Has the party moved down the beach?"

Dr. Philpott awkwardly stepped to shield the body of Florence Adams from his wife's view.

Mrs. Philpott stopped, her thick ankles sinking into the sand. "Mel, what's the matter with you?"

"Shirley, prepare yourself."

Mrs. Philpott's eyes grew wary. In a very unladylike manner, she pushed her husband out of the way, then abruptly stopped, nearly toppling over. Her pudgy hand clutched at pearls.

"No, no, no. It can't be!"

In the glow of twilight, Rosa could see that Shirley Philpott had lost color.

"I just talked to her not a half an hour ago," Mrs.

Philpott said and burst into tears. "H . . . how did this happen? How could it happen! Did she drown? Was she drunk again? Did she have a heart attack? This is just awful." She let out a loud, mournful sob. "*Awfuuuull!*"

Aunt Louisa grabbed Mrs. Philpott by the shoulders, and to Rosa's astonishment, shook the grieved woman.

"Get yourself together, Shirley. You aren't helping anyone by falling apart."

Mrs. Philpott responded to the admonishment, and, with a twinge of admiration, Rosa watched her aunt as she led Mrs. Philpott away.

Dr. Philpott looked equally grateful as he pulled his gaze away from his wife and back to the body before him. "I'm going to need my bag to start documenting," he said. "I'm not the one to lead this, since, obviously, I have a conflict of interest, but since I'm already here, I'll start."

"I'll get one of my band members to fetch it," Miguel said.

"Thanks." Dr. Philpott let out a long sigh. "That will probably be a lot faster than if I went myself." He shook his head. "Brown Chevrolet two-door sedan. The bag is in the trunk." He threw a set of keys to Miguel, who caught them.

Miguel nodded, "I'll be right back."

Having passed the distraught Mrs. Philpott on to someone else, Aunt Louisa caught up to Rosa again.

"Are you all right, Rosa?"

"Yes, I'm fine. How about you?

Aunt Louisa straightened her dress. "As well as can be expected. I've told the caterers to clean up. This event has been ruined. Thoroughly ruined."

Nothing like a dead body to kill the fun.

Aunt Louisa waved her hand at the scene on the beach. "It wouldn't be the first time someone drank too much and fell off a pier."

"I overheard Mrs. Philpott ask Miss Adams if she was drunk again," Rosa stated.

"Yes," Aunt Louisa said with a nod. "Flo drinks . . . drank too much at parties . . . and other things too. I don't see the point in denying that." She paused, and Rosa thought that her aunt would actually show emotion, but instead, she grew indignant. "I mean, how could she?"

"What did you mean by other things?" Rosa asked. "Are you implying that she was taking illegal drugs?"

"Well, I don't think it was like street drugs." Aunt Louisa patted the bottom of her hair and adjusted her hat. "Not cocaine or heroin or anything like that, but maybe prescription drugs or something. I don't really know. I don't think anyone really knows, including her cousin Shirley. I mean Flo is . . . was a bit of a loner."

Red flashing lights signaled that the police had arrived, and several officers hurried to the beach. Rosa reflexively looked for Raul Mendez, the accountant who had run to phone the police, but he was not with them.

Dr. Philpott had taken a camera from a large leather bag and took pictures of the body from several angles. The flashes from the bulb lit up the entire scene as he circled the body. He directed his comments to Miguel. "Seeing how we don't know if this is a homicide or just a freak drowning accident," he said, "I'm assuming you don't mind if I snap a few more pictures. I will hand them over to Dr. Rayburn if needed."

Kneeling to examine the body again, Dr. Philpott slowly opened Florence Adams' mouth with the end of a pencil. His eyebrows were furrowed as he gently pressed down on her chest. "Hmmm."

"What is it?" Miguel asked.

"Well, if she drowned . . ." He glanced at Miguel, but just shrugged his shoulders, then looked at Rosa, "You found the body first, didn't you?"

Rosa broke in. "There was no seawater. I turned the body on its side to clear the airway in case she was still alive. There was no water."

"You're sure, young lady?" the pathologist asked.

Rosa nodded. "Yes."

With a grunt, Dr. Philpott braced his back and

stood. "We'll have to wait to see what Dr. Rayburn finds before making any conclusions." He paused, let out another sigh, took off his glasses, and rubbed the bridge of his nose. "Normally, one would expect water to be present in the lungs in a drowning death."

He locked eyes with Miguel. "Mick, I think you should treat this as a suspicious death."

$\mathcal{T}$wo officers approached. "Detective Belmonte," one of them started. "Dispatch said you were on the scene already."

"Thanks for getting here so fast, Officer Jenkins." Miguel turned to Rosa. "Let's talk later, okay?"

"Okay," she said. The single word came out, not in the firm, authoritative way, Rosa had wanted, but as a whimper. Her heart betrayed her as she watched Miguel walk away, by doing heavy somersaults. Rosa chastised herself and her dumb body for its involuntary reactions. Her face felt hot with a dreadful blush. After all these years, Miguel Belmonte had the worst effect on her.

Rosa returned to what was left of the party. It had been a bizarre evening, and her emotions felt as taut as a piano wire. First, being thrust into a Forrester family charity event, then the dead body on the beach, and finally, seeing Miguel in such an intense context—it was rather overwhelming.

Rosa walked the beach in search of Gloria to tell her she'd take a taxi back to the Forrester mansion. She found her cousin sitting on a lawn chair in quiet conversation with the young lady, Vanessa, who'd discovered the body. Vanessa held a tissue in one hand and dabbed her eyes.

Gloria had her arm around the woman but stood up as Rosa approached. "It's been a bit emotional tonight. Especially for Vanessa." Gloria gestured towards the woman. "I don't think you've met her. Vanessa is Clarence's wife."

"Oh?" The connection surprised Rosa. What an odd coincidence that the person who found the body was someone she should've known, who was in fact related by marriage. However, Rosa never made it to cousin Clarence's wedding, and had never made his wife's acquaintance.

"Actually, ex-wife, but don't say that too loud," Gloria said, lowering her voice.

Rosa remembered receiving a letter from Gloria telling her that the marriage hadn't lasted.

"Mom insists they try to behave, at least in public," Gloria said. "For the sake of the family's repu-tation. Occasionally, Vanessa plays along." Like a balloon with a slow leak, Gloria sighed long and slowly.

"Vanessa, this is my cousin Rosa. She lived with us during the war. Rosa, this is Vanessa Forrester."

Rosa and Vanessa studied one another, both knowing that the other knew about their mutual marital failures—Vanessa's divorce and Rosa's altar run. Gloria could keep a secret if she wanted to, but that desire rarely surfaced.

"Hello," Rosa said.

Vanessa offered a weak smile. "Hi."

Facing Rosa, Gloria said, "I'm guessing you're ready to go home, right?"

"I wouldn't mind," Rosa admitted. "Is there a phone booth nearby to call a cab?"

"I'll drive you. I've had quite enough for one night too."

Vanessa shifted in her chair, and Gloria said, "We're going to go now. Should I find Clarence?"

Vanessa shook her head. "I came with a friend. I've got a ride."

"We'll see you then." Gloria gave her former sister-in-law a quick hug. "Stay strong."

Rosa and Gloria walked to the parking lot, the car keys jingling in Gloria's hand.

"Poor girl," Gloria said. "Such a shock to find a dead body."

"Was she questioned?" Rosa asked. Miguel had stepped away from the scene for a brief time, and she wondered if he'd tracked her down. It's what Rosa would have done were she the lead in the investigation.

"Yes, but it was a quick interview. Vanessa really didn't have much information. She was walking along the beach, staring into the sunset, and almost stumbled over the body. She screamed, of course. Well, I guess you know the rest."

After returning to the Forrester mansion, Rosa took a long bath in the oversized porcelain soaking tub in the bathroom attached to her bedroom which had been updated with soothing sea foam green and black tiles. She almost fell asleep as she soaked. It took some willpower to climb out, but afterwards, she dried off, put on her silk nightgown, and collapsed into her king-sized canopied bed. It felt luxurious to be horizontal on a comfortable mattress. Her bags remained only half unpacked on the marble floor beside the bed.

As she drifted off, the vision of Lord Winston Eveleigh at an altar passed through her mind's eye. It morphed suddenly into the image of a Latino man wearing cotton chinos with a guitar strapped over his shoulder. A smile formed on her face as she drifted into sleep.

. . .

A BLAST of sunshine through her window woke Rosa the next morning. Southern California mornings were bright, and she pinched her eyes against the glare and vowed to close the curtains that night.

The hands on the round-faced alarm clock indicated it was only six a.m.; however, she calculated that she had gotten around seven hours of uninterrupted sleep. For the moment, she felt quite rested, but she also knew that a wave of fatigue would likely hit her in the afternoon. To speed up acclimatizing to Pacific Standard Time, she would have to resist the powerful urge to nap.

Using her toes, she located her slippers that stuck out from under the bed. Rosa headed down the vast staircase and through a wide corridor to the kitchen in search of something for breakfast. The staff at the Forrester mansion had yet to arrive, but she was too famished to wait. Upon opening the refrigerator, she saw a large container filled with homemade Mexican-style granola. She remembered the Forresters' chief housekeeper, Señora Gomez, had a delicious recipe, and Rosa's stomach almost leapt for joy when she saw it. It always tasted superb when mixed with blueberries and fresh milk.

After pouring a glass of fresh orange juice, she found a serving tray and carried her full glass and bowl across the terra-cotta tiled floor to the morning room.

Like the morning room at Hartigan House, Rosa's home in Kensington, the sliding glass doors opened to the back garden.

As a teenager, the patio had been her favorite place to sit and have breakfast. It overlooked a tennis court, a huge flower garden that featured a terraced lawn with carefully manicured hedges, and a large kidney-shaped swimming pool with a beautiful stonework deck, which was surrounded by padded lounging chairs. Three tiled Mediterranean-style water fountains with the soothing sound of trickling water greeted her as she stepped outside into the warming air. The sun cast the whole scene with a golden filter.

Palm trees, planted in a border around the yard, swayed gently in the warm breeze. From the pool, one could enjoy a view of the town below and just beyond that, lay the Pacific Ocean, which sparkled in perfect blue in the early morning sunshine. Rosa felt a sense of contentment rush over her. It would be a gorgeous day.

Claiming a cedar wood pool lounger, Rosa took a sip of orange juice and, closing her eyes, felt the warmth of the sun on her face. After Aunt Louisa's comment on her pale English skin, she was determined to get a tan, even if it meant an unleashing of freckles. She was glad she'd come to California and sighed contentedly.

Then as if a curtain were quickly drawn, the

memory of the shocking turn of events from the night before returned. Her eyes snapped opened.

She must still be suffering from jet lag to have such a dramatic event slip her mind, or maybe her hunger pangs had taken her focus. A lady had died, which was tragic, but Rosa didn't have the authority of WPC Reed in California. She had no investigative rights here, and she'd do herself a big favor by turning off her compulsion to butt in.

Not to mention how unsettling it had been to run into Miguel Belmonte. She and Miguel had lost touch after the war—despite initial promises to keep writing— and Rosa had thought he'd be living in his home city, Los Angeles. She'd never expected that he'd settled in Santa Bonita, and she certainly hadn't known he'd joined the police force, much less made the rank of detective.

Rosa exhaled through pursed lips. None of this had occurred to her when she had impulsively flown to California.

"Hola, señorita!" Señora Gomez's cheerful voice rang out across the garden.

Pulled out of her reverie, Rosa smiled at the familiar figure, older now, and rounder in the face and the hips. The Forrester family's long-standing house-keeper had smooth brown skin, sparkling dark eyes, and long black hair now showing some gray and tied back in a bun. She carried a tray set with a small silver coffee urn and containers for cream and sugar, which she lowered onto the table next to Rosa.

"Buenos dias, señorita!"

"Buenos dias."

The housekeeper's gaze dropped to Rosa's bowl of cereal sitting on the table. "I'm glad you enjoy my granola, Miss Rosa."

"It's the best."

Señora Gomez cupped her hands at her waist and studied Rosa with an appraising look. "Look at you. *Una mujer muy hermosa!* A very beautiful woman! *Si?*"

Rosa laughed, well aware that her face was bare and her hair mussed and unbrushed.

Despite this, the housekeeper gushed, "Oh, señorita, you will have every young man in Santa Bonita at your command, no? So slender. Maybe too slender, no? No matter. *Muy bien.* I heard about what happened in London, you don't worry about anything. I'll take care of you. My cooking has healed broken hearts before." She gave Rosa's cheek a pinch. Something she used to do often.

For a moment, Rosa felt fifteen again.

"Please enjoy your coffee, Miss Rosa. Mrs. Hartigan is on her way out to visit with you." She smiled warmly, lifted Rosa's empty granola bowl, then turned back towards the house.

Rosa took off her slippers and padded over to the pool, bent down to sit on the edge, and dipped her feet in the warm, clear water.

"Good morning, Rosa," her grandmother said, her Bostonian accent filtering through. Rosa smiled over her shoulder toward the voice. Her grandmother, Sally Hartigan, had grown frailer over the last eleven years, but as a lady in her eighth decade, she still carried herself with a certain grace. Wearing a simple summer dress in a good-quality floral print cotton that hugged her ample bosom and the plump curves of her hips, she slowly made her way from the house to the pool area.

Rosa clasped the elderly woman's wrinkled hand. "Did you sleep well, Grandma Sally?"

Rosa had mistakenly called Sally Hartigan "Grandmother", and had been firmly admonished and accused of being "thoroughly British".

Sally Hartigan wasn't Rosa's grandmother by blood. She had been her maternal grandfather's second wife, and stepmother to Rosa's mother, Ginger.

"I slept. I'm getting old, of course, but that can't be avoided."

Rosa helped her get seated at the patio table and then sat across from her. Grandma Sally pursed her lined lips, and the wrinkles around her eyes deepened.

"I'm desperately curious, you know, and I hope you've been here long enough that I'm not violating social protocol—I know how important that is to you Brits— but could you tell me what happened?"

About the death the night before? Rosa felt her expression crinkle in confusion. How was asking about that breaking protocol? Perhaps the elderly lady's mind was slipping.

As if she could read Rosa's *mind*, Grandma Sally snorted. "About your nuptials. I'm sorry I couldn't make the journey to London, it's a bit much for these old bones, but . . . can you tell me what happened?"

Rosa sighed, leaned back in her chair, and let her arms drop loosely on her lap. *Oh, that.*

Her grandmother didn't seem to notice her obvious reluctance, or if she did, dismissed it out of hand. She pressed on, "It seemed like such a good match, you and that Lord Winston Eveleigh fellow. I mean, I know your mother had certain reservations bu—"

"My mother was right," Rosa interrupted. "I should have taken more heed of her advice. I almost made a huge mistake, Grandma Sally. I really don't want to talk about it right now."

Disappointment flashed behind her grandmother's watery blue eyes. "Of course." She sat back, straightened as much as one with aged shoulders such as she had, could. "I understand, dear. Well, maybe time spent breathing in the Pacific air will help you put it all behind you."

"I hope so." Rosa felt bad about not giving her grandmother what she wanted. Perhaps she'd be enticed by a possible murder investigation.

"Did you hear about last night?"

Grandma Sally lowered her chin. "Louisa told me all about it when she got in. I couldn't sleep, so I made the mistake of coming down into the kitchen just as she got home. She was upset. Terrible, just terrible. To think this kind of thing could happen in this little town. Now Boston, that's a different story." Grandma Sally's gaze drifted to the distance, and the subtle smile that pulled on her wrinkled lips made Rosa believe the elderly lady had more fond memories of New England than not.

"I don't really remember Aunt Louisa being involved in charity work when I was here last time," Rosa said. Uncharitably, Rosa wouldn't have pegged her aunt as the philanthropist type.

"Well, that was during the war, mind you. There were lots of other things going on. But yes, organizing charity drives has become a new passion of hers— unlikely as it sounds. Though they don't seem to last long. There was the Santa Bonita Society for the Preservation of Animals which she raved about until a puppy peed in her lap at a rally." Grandma Sally's lined lips tugged up into a grin as she recalled the incident.

"Yes, that was the end of that. Then there was the Society for Santa Bonita Public Library, but that ended over a disagreement she had with the head librarian, Miss Cumberbatch."

Rosa's mind stuttered at Grandma Sally's innocent mention of the local library. It was the one place in Santa Bonita that—despite Rosa's love of reading and discovering intriguing bits of trivia—she'd vowed never to step foot into again. Her memories and emotions attached to that place and the park it nestled against were too strong, and she had Miguel to blame for that.

"... after that, she took over as president of the local Santa Bonita Women's League..."

Rosa blinked forcing her mind back to the present and on Grandma Sally's recitation of Aunt Louisa's trail of dissatisfying ventures.

"... until she resigned two years ago—she got offended by a remark someone made at a fundraising dinner. Then there was the United Way, and she was asked to leave after one year. I never did find out why. My daughter can be very closed-lipped when she wants to be."

Rosa nodded politely.

"Now, this charity for Polio, which, as far as I understand, exists to raise money for polio victims. I can applaud Louisa's desire to do some good in the world when she has all this money, but she does like to be the center of attention."

Grandma Sally removed a handkerchief she had tucked in the cuff of one sleeve and dabbed at her eyes that watered in the brightness of the morning sun. "I always tell her to let some of it go. After she lost Harold, she immersed herself in his business affairs, so this passion for charities seems frivolous to me. Quite honestly, I don't know what she's trying to prove."

Harold Forrester, Rosa's uncle, had died during the war. Rosa remembered how distraught Aunt Louisa had been when she'd heard the news. She had had a hard time coming to grips with this tragedy. Besides the obvious heartache she suffered, it had also seemed inconceivable to her aunt that someone so rich and powerful would've been put in harm's way, or could die.

Rosa poured a glass of orange juice for Sally Hartigan, who gave her a look of gratitude before drinking.

Her grandmother carefully set the glass on the table, then continued, "I hope I don't sound callous. I understand the loss and emptiness a person can feel at the loss of a spouse. I lost my George long ago, back in 1923, and sometimes it feels like yesterday. But I didn't try to be someone I wasn't to forget him."

Rosa had never met her grandfather. He died

before her mother and father had even met, and he was rarely spoken about, though Rosa's mother only had kind things to say when words were said about him.

"What was he like?" she asked.

"Who?"

"Grandpa Hartigan."

Sally Hartigan's eyes grew soft with remembering. "He was older than me by quite a bit. Twenty-five years, in fact, twice my age. Perhaps I missed my own father. He passed away when I was just a girl. I can't really say why I was drawn to George, but I was. He was kind, intelligent, very good at business. Some accused me of marrying him for money, but that was only partly true. I loved him, dearly."

Rosa blinked at Grandma Sally's admitting she'd married George Hartigan for money, even in part. But, in those days, a woman had to do what she had to do to survive, Rosa supposed. She was glad to hear love had been part of the equation.

"I'm sorry he was taken from you so soon," she said.

"It was a dreadful disease, and a horrible time watching him die a little every day. It was very hard on Louisa. Oh, she likes to act like she's a terribly strong person. I think it was her way of coping with life without her father."

Rosa felt honored that Grandma Sally was

confiding in her in this way and determined to be a little easier on Aunt Louisa.

Grandma Sally moved to stand up, and Rosa rose to help her.

"Anyway," Grandma Sally started, "I better get ready. We have a visitor coming soon."

Rosa raised a brow. "Oh?"

"Yes, that young Latino police detective is apparently coming by this morning to talk about what happened last night and . . . oh, I didn't mean to startle you."

A rush of blood made Rosa feel off balance. *Miguel was coming here?* She blinked rapidly to regain her composure. "Um . . . I have to . . . I mean, it was nice chatting, Grandma Sally. I'll see you later."

Rosa darted back into the house, skirted the dining room, and ran up the wide staircase, puffing. She was quite out of breath when she reached her room. She had no makeup on, and her hair was a mess, and worst of all, she was still in her pajamas and her housecoat! Miguel was coming! As her mother liked to say, oh mercy!

4

*S*hortly after Rosa had arrived at Forrester
mansion, one of the maids, Darla—Rosa was
determined to learn all their names—had ironed and
then hung her dresses in the built-in closet. They had
only wooden wardrobes back home at Hartigan House.
Though there were many similarities in the two large
homes—entrances with high ceilings, large, curving
staircases to the second floor, grand living rooms,
dining rooms, morning rooms, and mature gardens,
along with a full staff including housekeeper, cook, and
gardener, there were many differences. Where
Hartigan House was made of stone and had been
standing for over a hundred years, the Forrester
mansion was a newer wood-frame construct with a
facade of white stucco. The gardens in England were

typical for climates that enjoyed four seasons but lacked the dynamic and playful additions of palm trees and citrus plants.

None of these things was on Rosa's mind which swirled in a state of irrational panic as she flipped through her dresses, unable to decide on what to wear to her first nonpublic encounter with Miguel.

Her heart raced. When she'd flown into Santa Bonita, she couldn't stop the memories of her time spent here previously, which had included Miguel Belmonte, but she hadn't anticipated seeing him again. He was supposed to be safely ensconced in Los Angeles.

Oh dear.

Mid-decade fashions for dresses were quite unified —some variation of a full skirt, a belted waist, and fitted bodice. The differences lay in the fabric, color, design, and type of sleeve—three-quarter length, capped, or without.

Rosa finally settled on a jade-green dress, no pattern, with matching green buttons that ran from her cleavage to the hem. A matching green belt brought the outfit together. It was simple, yet elegant, not too loud, but classy. And green always brought out the best in her eyes. Rosa brushed her hair and pulled it from her face with a hairband. Finally, she added tasteful pearl stud earrings and a pearl choker necklace.

Oh, did she look too sophisticated? Did this dress make her look older than her twenty-eight years? If only Gloria was awake, she'd get her advice. Staring at her image in the mirror, she chastised herself. She was overthinking this. Miguel wasn't coming to take her on a date. He might not even want to see her.

She was *overthinking* this.

A knock on the door produced Aunt Louisa. "Good, you're awake and dressed. That Mexican detective is here, asking questions about Florence." She frowned. "For some reason, he wants to see you, though I can't think why. You didn't know Flo, and you've only just arrived." Aunt Louisa's right eye twitched. "Should I tell him you're indisposed?"

Rosa wasn't fooled. Aunt Louisa knew full well who Detective Belmonte was and was likely afraid to leave Rosa alone in the same room with him.

"I'm a trained police officer," Rosa said, unnecessarily, "and I was one of the first at the scene."

"It's all rather moot, isn't it?" Aunt Louisa said. "Flo drank too much and fell off the pier. It's tragic but hardly unusual."

"I'm sure he's only after my professional impressions."

Aunt Louisa narrowed her eyes suspiciously, then walked away. Rosa called after her, "Where is he?"

Her aunt spoke without looking back. "Front parlor."

Rosa's heart drummed in her chest most annoyingly. She felt like a schoolgirl being picked up for a prom, rather than a professional about to speak to another professional. Before she entered the front parlor, she put her shoulders back, took a deep fortifying breath, and told herself, "I'm Woman Police Constable Reed of the London Metropolitan Police. I'm confident and trained. I'm the daughter of Ginger Reed."

Miguel sat on the sectional couch, his legs crossed, and his dark eyes studying a notebook. He wore a detective's plainclothes uniform of trousers—or as she was now in America—*pants* and suit jacket, with a white shirt and blue tie. When he saw her, he stood, his hat in hand. Rosa and Miguel stared at each for an awkward moment.

"Well, this is sure a surprise," Miguel remarked. "How long has it been since you were last in Santa Bonita?"

Did he not remember? She, for one, would never forget. "Eleven years."

Rosa wondered if he would offer his hand or perhaps an embrace between old friends, but the tear in their relationship was too ragged.

Rosa fanned out her skirt, sat down gracefully—the

way her mother had taught her—and crossed her ankles to one side. Miguel stared as she did this, and then seeming to catch himself, he returned to his seat on the sofa.

He tipped his chin. "I've heard you've become a police officer too?"

"Yes. You might remember that my mother has an investigation agency in London. My father was a superintendent at Scotland Yard until his retirement, so I guess you could say the apple didn't fall far from the tree."

"Oh, yes, I remember that."

There was a moment of awkward silence until Miguel cleared his throat and recited a short account of his history. "I entered the academy in Los Angeles a few months after the war, then worked as a patrol officer for some years. Later, when I was promoted to detective, I was transferred here to Santa Bonita."

The air was thick with questions neither dared to ask, such as *Did you marry? Are there children?*

Miguel pulled at his collar to loosen his tie. "Do you mind if I ask you a few questions about yesterday?"

"Go ahead."

"Did you see anyone you would call suspicious last night? I know you don't know many people, but given your training, you may have noticed something. I should tell you that we are tentatively treating this death as suspicious. At least, until the official pathology report."

"I may have noticed a few things," Rosa said as Miguel opened his notebook again. "I witnessed a heated exchange between Shirley Philpott and Florence Adams not long before the body was found. I couldn't hear what it was about, but it took place away from the main party. I did hear Florence yelling at the end of it. She said her drink was empty, and she needed more."

Miguel scratched at his notebook. "How long was this before the body was found?"

"I would guess not more than half an hour."

"And did Miss Adams appear intoxicated to you?"

"Actually, she did appear tipsy when Aunt Louisa introduced her to me when I first arrived at the party."

Miguel nodded and continued to write. "Anything else?"

"A few minutes after the argument, I saw Miss Adams meet up with a man on the opposite side of the pier. I'd started walking along the shore when I came upon them. The sun was almost down on the horizon, so I didn't get a clear look at him. I saw him try to kiss her—"

Inexplicably, Rosa's gaze landed on Miguel's lips. How often had she kissed them! Those adorable

dimples jumped out at her. She
into her hand.

Drat! She felt a flare of red
Had Miguel caught her staring

"And?" Miguel prompted.

Swallowing hard, Rosa ma
forced herself to remain professional. "And then she
rebuffed him and started back in the direction of the
party again."

Miguel hummed and jotted her story down. "Is
there anything else? Can you describe the man who
tried to kiss Florence?"

Rosa thought back. "Like I said, I didn't get a good
look at him. He had medium-length hair which he
wore loosely without any oil or it being slicked back, at
least it blew in the breeze, so I'm assuming so. He was
lean and wore a loose Hawaiian floral shirt."

"Very good," Miguel said appreciatively. "Obviously, you have an eye for detail."

"One more thing." Rosa raised a finger. "I saw him
standing at the very edge of the crowd when the body
was found. He seemed to notice me looking at him and
then disappeared. What I find odd is that he left before
anyone knew whose body was on the beach."

Miguel agreed. "That is unusual." He slipped his
notepad into his suit pocket and surprised Rosa with a

bject. "How long are you planning to stay

Bonita?"

My return date is yet to be determined."

"No family to get back to? You never married?"

He dared to ask the questions!

A knot formed in Rosa's stomach. She couldn't very well tell him she'd recently left a good man at the altar. And at twenty-eight years of age, she had no other prospects. Many people considered her on the verge of spinsterhood.

"No," she said simply. "You?"

"Engaged." He seemed to watch Rosa for her reaction. She kept her expression impassive though her emotions were an inner storm. *Of course, he was,* she thought to herself. She was surprised he wasn't already married with a bunch of children clinging to his legs.

"Congratulations." It came out dryly, and before she could check herself she asked, "Who's the lucky girl?"

Miguel held her gaze for a moment too long before answering. "Her name is Charlene. Charlene Winters. She's an aspiring actress and lives, for the time being, in Los Angeles."

"I see." Rosa was dying to know more, especially about how their long-distance relationship was working, and then chided herself. It was none of her business. She'd lost all rights to know anything about

Miguel's life when she left him—refusing his proposal —to return to London in '45.

Miguel smoothed out his slacks and stood. "I need to get going. I was hoping to interview Mr. Clarence Forrester and Miss Gloria Forrester, but your aunt tells me they are still asleep. I guess I came a bit early in the day." He smiled, and this time Rosa was ready for the dimples.

"No need to show me out," he said. "I can find my way. I'll be back sometime over the next couple of days."

After he left, Rosa found her way to the rear garden again, feeling emotionally drained. She'd thought she'd pass through the rest of her life without ever setting eyes on Miguel Belmonte again, chalking up that tumultuous time—four measly months out of her twenty-eight years—to a youthful, emotional lapse. Seeing Miguel again was like awakening Mount Vesuvius, or rousing Old Faithful. Oh, what a dreadful turn of events!

Aunt Louisa approached with an iced tea in each hand. She handed one to Rosa.

"The two of you must've had a lot to say."

Rosa plopped onto a pool lounger. "We only spoke about the case, Auntie."

Aunt Louisa gracefully lowered herself into a nearby patio chair. "I would assume nothing else."

45

"They're considering the death suspicious."

Aunt Louisa turned sharply. "You can't be serious."

"Detective Belmonte was quite serious."

Aunt Louisa sipped on her iced tea, deep in thought. "*Detective* Belmonte will do his best, I'm sure," she said, sounding platitudinal, "but there aren't many *suspicious deaths* in Santa Bonita. I personally have my doubts that *he* is experienced enough to solve a homicide. I know this sounds terribly insensitive, but the truth is, people of his ethnicity have a harder time in positions of authority."

Not sure what to make of that statement, Rosa furrowed her eyebrows.

Her aunt continued, "Well, you see people who are . . . like us, dear, may be reluctant to discuss every detail with a *Hispanic* man. Not everyone is as open-minded as you and me, Rosa."

Rosa choked on her iced tea. Aunt Louisa's view of herself was stunning.

Her aunt frowned in her direction. "Are you all right?"

"Yes. Sorry."

Aunt Louisa continued her monologue. "It just may be that he'll have a harder time getting to the real truth of it." She took a sip of her tea. "Frankly, I think you have more experience. And look at your pedigree."

Rosa's parentage was common knowledge to the

Forrester family, but what they didn't know, what almost no one knew, was that her mother had been a secret agent during the First World War. Rosa only knew about her mother's secret and often dangerous life because she'd happened upon an old journal where her mother had, selectively and roughly coded, recorded some of her exploits. Rosa suspected that both of her parents had been recruited by the crown during the last war.

"Rosa? Are you listening?"

Rosa snapped back to attention. "Yes, Aunt Louisa."

"I think you'd do a better job."

Aunt Louisa's statement was preposterous. "I don't have jurisdiction in California. I doubt anyone would appreciate a police officer from another country interfering." *Much less a female officer*, but Rosa kept that unsavory sentiment to herself.

Aunt Louisa's lips twitched. She stood and patted Rosa on the shoulder. "I have some pull with the mayor. Just leave it to me."

"Aunt Louisa! You mustn't."

"Of course, I must. I mean . . . there are a few details that I would rather keep 'in-house', you might say. Besides, you're bound to get bored with no grand puzzle to solve."

Rosa's mouth dropped open as she watched her

aunt walk away armed with a new project—her pumps clicking on the tile as she strutted away, her shoulders straight with confidence.

Rosa would've laughed if she didn't know her aunt better. Louisa Hartigan Forrester was a force to be reckoned with, and the kind of lady who fully expected to get her way.

5

*R*osa spent the rest of the day trying to relax and recharge her mental and physical batteries. When Gloria finally got out of bed, they spent time lounging around the pool. Rosa was glad she'd brought her swimming suit along, but if she were to stay much longer, she'd buy something a little more in vogue. Perhaps something from the Egyptian Collection on the cover of the *Cole California* magazine Gloria was currently reading. She liked the lemon-yellow one with diagonal hieroglyphic ribbons. Gloria looked especially charming, in her red suit with contrasting white piping and large four-hole white buttons on the shoulders.

It seemed they were both determined not to bring up the unpleasantness of the night before, and the subject of Florence Adams' death never came up.

Instead, they discussed the up-and-coming music star with the unusual name, Elvis—and yes, Rosa thought him to be ravishingly attractive.

Gloria looked up from the magazine which had fallen open on her lap. "I look at you and think, if I don't get married, I'd really like to do something with my life. I just can't think of what. I lack purpose."

"You can do something with your life even if you do marry."

"Oh, you know what I mean. It's just, I don't know what I want to do with my life. Did you always want to join the police?"

Rosa considered her cousin's question. Had she? It wasn't something she'd thought about when she'd lived in California in the forties. What had she wanted back then?

"I don't think I knew what I wanted until after the war." She'd spent several weeks feeling entirely out of place in London and was almost crippled by the pain of missing Miguel. It took serious effort to keep the British "stiff upper lip" in working order. But after a year of mourning her losses, she rediscovered her love of London.

"I remember watching my mother solve a case. She'd recruited me to help at her office of Lady Gold Investigations." Rosa knew it was her mother's attempt at bringing her back to life and out of her mental slump. She'd eventually confided in her the nature of her melancholy. "You need to keep your mind busy," her mother had said. "I'll teach you how to develop photos in the dark room."

"It was during that time when I recognized my aptitude," Rosa continued. "My father confirmed my feelings by suggesting the Metropolitan Police Training School. They were actively recruiting women for the force. The war had changed the way society looked at women, and employment options other than nursing and teaching became possible."

Gloria moaned. "That's what I don't know. My aptitudes." She whipped her sunglasses off and stared hard at Rosa. "Can you tell? What do you think my aptitudes are?"

Rosa pushed her own sunglasses more tightly to her face and hoped Gloria didn't see her look of distress. How was she to answer that? Certainly not driving. Or working anywhere that required one to stay silent.

"Rosa?"

"I'm thinking."

Rosa reclined on the lounger and propped up a knee. "There are a great many things you could do."

"Like?"

"Well, you could follow in your mother's footsteps and promote charities."

"Oh, I suppose. I'd just like to do something—"

"That your mother's not doing?"

"Yes. Thank you for understanding. I know you and your mom are close, but my mother and I have a more complicated relationship."

Rosa could appreciate that. "Let's take some time to put our heads together. I'm sure we'll think of something that you'll want to do."

Gloria sipped on her drink. "It's so nice having you here, Rosa. We're like sisters! So much more fun."

Rosa held in the smile. She felt she'd burst into laughter if she wasn't careful. Gloria's outgoing personality was delightful. Her cousin had only been ten years old when Rosa left to go back to England, but despite their age difference, they'd spent quite a bit of time together.

As if to make sure Rosa was listening, Gloria eyed Rosa over her cat-eye sunglasses. "I love Clarence, but he can be such a pill. I mean, you know what brothers are like, right? How is Scout, by the way? I barely had a chance to speak to him in London."

Scout, who went by Samuel now, was Rosa's older brother.

"He's very busy with his horses."

"Still racing?"

"Yes, though I warn him he's getting a little old to keep withstanding the rigors necessary to be a jockey. I tell him he should trade in his horses for a wife and family," Rosa huffed, "but who am I to talk?"

Gloria patted Rosa's hand. "Oh, you'll find the right man one day, don't you worry." Rosa's mind immediately betrayed her by going to Miguel. Her face grew warm and she flapped her hands, pretending to be succumbing to the midday heat.

Gloria threw her thin legs over the edge of her lounger. "I'm feeling hungry, anyway. It must be lunchtime soon. We can eat inside for a change."

ROSA AND GLORIA changed into summer dresses for the afternoon and met again in the dining room for lunch. Señora Gomez produced a plate of tacos—Rosa did miss Mexican food. When she tried to explain the spicy mix of flavors to her British counterparts, she received deep frowns and looks of distrust. The British preferred their food plain and simple.

Clarence—looking very much like an American businessman—sauntered in as they were finishing. He wore a red tie and a starchy white shirt tucked into high-waisted, pleated pants with cuffs that rested on leather loafers.

"Vanessa called. She's dropping Julie off this afternoon."

Julie was Clarence's four-year-old daughter.

"I'm looking forward to meeting her," Rosa said.

"Actually," Clarence's eyes registered an idea, "I was wondering if you and Gloria would like to take her out, do girl things."

"I love my niece," Gloria said, "but I think she'd rather spend time with her dad."

"I know, and we will. It's just that I have an awful lot of work to do."

Gloria's expression was just short of ridicule. "What 'work' do you do?"

He scowled at her. "I run Dad's business affairs. You don't know everything I do. There's a lot more to it than meets the eye."

Rosa had learned from her mother that Clarence had been "officially" put in charge of his father's vast business holdings, but it was Aunt Louisa who sat on the board and called the shots.

Rosa pitied Clarence. It would be difficult for him to fill his father's shoes if his mother insisted on wearing them instead.

"Let's take Julie for ice cream," Rosa offered. "I wouldn't mind doing a bit of shopping,"

Gloria sent Rosa a pointed look. "You could use a few items more appropriate for our weather. And Santa Bonita has several high-quality clothing shops now. Very modern American."

Rosa also wanted to see about buying a pair of

Riviera sunglasses. She had recently spied a pair in a catalogue that featured rhinestones and gilded charms on the frames. Besides, one pair of sunglasses for California wasn't nearly enough.

"By the way," Gloria said as she pushed a half-empty plate away. "There's a variety show playing at the American Legion Hall tonight. Mick and The Beat Boys are playing a set." When Rosa failed to register the group's name, Gloria explained. "That's Detective Belmonte's group. You saw them last night. Wouldn't it be fun to see them playing some rock and roll instead of that Sinatra stuff they played at the polio event?"

Gloria misunderstood Rosa's hesitation. Their age difference meant that Gloria hadn't been privy to Rosa and Miguel's intense, but short-lived relationship. The thought of seeing Miguel again, especially with his band, filled her with a mixture of emotions she couldn't even put a name to, but Gloria's enthusiastic insistence was unstoppable.

"Come on, Rosa. It'll be fun. I can introduce you around."

"Won't Detective Belmonte be busy? With the . . . er . . . case?"

"I don't think a drowning will keep him from playing his guitar. He's an excellent musician, you know? If he weren't taken, I'd make a move on him myself."

Rosa suddenly found it hard to swallow. She sipped on her glass of iced tea, then, as nonchalantly as possible, asked, "You've met his girlfriend?"

"I've seen her on TV."

Rosa hated the heavy pit that formed in her stomach. She didn't even want to examine what had caused it. Was it because Miguel had a girlfriend, or that he had a pretty girlfriend on television?

"She's in one of those Clairol commercials, you know?" Gloria continued. " *Does she?...Or doesn't she?*" She laughed at the innuendo. "Charlene Winters is stunning blond, even in black and white." She smirked and arched a brow in Rosa's direction. "And I think she *does*."

Oh dear! The thought of what that might mean made Rosa feel sick to her stomach. Now she wished lunch had been plain English food and not spicy foreign fare.

Impervious to Rosa's discomfort, Gloria said, "It's just a fantasy. Mom would kill me if I actually brought a man like Detective Belmonte home."

Rosa didn't doubt that.

"But—" Gloria poked Rosa in the arm. "You know what? I could be an actress on TV! I'm just as glamorous as Charlene Winters." Gloria patted the curls of her short and trendy hair do. "Don't you think? Though I know, I'm not as pretty."

Rosa had a feeling her attractive cousin was fishing for compliments. She allowed her one.

"You're just as pretty, and you know it. But it's not that easy, I don't think, to become a TV actress. I'm sure there's training you have to take." Rosa didn't know, but she was reasonably sure that Aunt Louisa wouldn't be in favor. Social propriety wasn't exclusive to the British, and in the minds of many upper-class people, an actress was only a step above a lady of the night.

"Maybe you're right," Gloria finally said. "I'm going to look into it. Anyway, you'll come with me? Tonight? To hear the band?"

Rosa couldn't think of a plausible reason to say no. "Sure."

LATER, Julie was unceremoniously dropped off at the front door into the care of Bledsoe, the butler, who took her by the hand and brought her to the kitchen where Gloria and Rosa were socializing.

Rosa looked at Gloria with raised eyebrows.

"Not an amicable relationship between Clarence and Vanessa, unfortunately," Gloria said in a hushed voice.

Soon after, the three drove into town in the Forresters' yellow and white, two-toned, automatic,

Chevrolet Bel Air sedan. Rosa admired the vehicle's glamorous long body and exaggerated tail fins.

Gloria cackled as they sped into town. "This car is Clarence's favorite. He'll fume when he sees it's gone, but serves him right for—" She tilted her head towards the backseat where little Julie played with a View Master toy. "—dodging his responsibilities."

Rosa held on to the hand strap attached to the car's ceiling and cast a concerned look at little Julie in the back seat. The small girl with neatly-styled blond ringlets tied with blue ribbons and wearing a sweet little sailor dress seemed unperturbed at her aunt's carefree driving and flashed her a chubby-faced smile.

In town, Gloria parked in front of an establishment Rosa hadn't seen before. A diamond-shaped, white-and-red checker sign had a white banner with the words "Tastee Freeze" written in blue. It was instantly cooler as they stepped into the air-conditioned shop where a small lineup of smiling people waited to order. Some were sitting on vinyl-covered bar stools eating their treats.

Over the counter, a large menu hung on the wall, depicting various treats that could be bought there. Some Rosa had never heard of before, such as the *Banana Royale* or the *Dip Top* Cone.

The Dip Top Cone turned out to be soft ice cream dipped into melted chocolate that dried to a shell as it cooled. Rosa and Julie both ordered one of those while Gloria ordered a hot caramel sundae. Rosa practically inhaled her soft cone. She'd never experienced ice cream like it before.

"Why don't you go on ahead," Gloria said after a while. "The stores are just down the street. Julie and I will catch up."

Rather than watch Julie's face become increasingly covered in melted ice cream, Rosa took Gloria up on her offer. A couple of blocks down Main Street, she came across a shop called *Pacific Trends* with some lovely designs for beach and casual wear. Rosa picked out a daring black two-piece bathing suit and the exact pair of sunglasses she had wanted.

Just as she was leaving the store, she spotted Shirley Philpott walking down the opposite sidewalk.

"Mrs. Philpott!"

Mrs. Philpott jerked toward Rosa's voice, then waved back, a quick, furtive gesture.

"Stay right there, I'll come over," Rosa called out, but the traffic was heavy. By the time she crossed the busy street, Shirley Philpott had disappeared. "Well, that is strange," Rosa muttered. She'd hoped to ask how the poor lady was faring after losing her cousin.

And perhaps a question or two about the dead woman.

6

*R*osa sat at the antique dressing table in her bedroom and stared back at her reflection in the oval mirror. She'd placed a wide, pink satin headband over her chestnut-colored hair—styled with tight curls pushed behind her ears—and held a tube of red lipstick. Her gaze latched on to the green eyes in the reflection of the oval mirror, and suddenly, it wasn't her mature, modern face looking back, but a rounder, youthful version, with long hair swooped into a fishnet hairpiece at the back of her head. The deep V of her neckline became a schoolgirl's outfit, but the blush on her cheeks was for the same boy.

Miguel Belmonte.

If she'd known he'd moved back to Santa Bonita, Rosa was sure she'd have chosen another destination to run away to. There was always the south of France, for instance—they had family friends there—or Boston, where Mum had acquaintances, or even to Canada.

Rosa let out a long breath. She knew no one in Canada, though she'd heard it was lovely, and indeed, was part of the Commonwealth, so she'd quite likely feel at home there.

But Rosa wasn't in those places. She was here, and so was Miguel. She'd just have to make the best of it.

Placing the lipstick pad on her lips, Rosa began to draw. The young lady she used to be no longer looked back at her. She was well and truly gone.

THE LOCAL AMERICAN LEGION HALL was a large, nicely painted wooden building that featured a large open room with oak parquet flooring. *A very American look*, Rosa thought. Not a single stone was used in its construction or any material over a hundred years old. Rows of foldable chairs were set out in front of a raised wooden stage area, and along one wall was a restaurant bar with round tables and booths. Hanging prominently on the wooden walls were black and white photographs of army battalions from both world wars, along with plaques commemorating various charities for which the organization had raised money.

After paying for their tickets at the entrance, Rosa and Gloria took a booth not far from the stage and ordered drinks. Rosa's only interest was to see one particular person's face, and though she tried to keep her search from looking obvious, Gloria was quick to notice her unrest.

"Who are you looking for?"

"No one. Just enjoying everyone's outfits."

The place quickly filled with people of all ages, but the majority were young people like Rosa and Gloria. Some young men sported pompadours. Others wore generously oiled 'duck tail' haircuts, while the ladies wore various styles of bouffant or waved coiffure styles.

But no Miguel.

Which was fine. No, good. Rosa told herself she hadn't come to see him anyway. She was only there at Gloria's request. Nothing more.

Various performers took the stage—a juggler, a folk music trio, and a young comedian. The crowd filled with laughter then applauded after the comedian Don Rickles finished his jokes.

"He's great!" Gloria said.

The 'headline' act, as everyone in the room knew, was Miguel's band, and yet Rosa still hadn't spotted him. Was he hiding out in a back room?

Her question was answered when the host took the microphone. "Ladies and Gentlemen, the advertised band for tonight is a local favorite, Mick and the Beat Boys. However, most of you know that Mick, otherwise known as local Detective Belmonte, was called away on important police business and couldn't make it tonight."

A groan went up from the crowd, and Gloria blew a loud raspberry through her full lips. "Figures."

Rosa felt a disarming mix of disappointment and relief. Not seeing Miguel again, *ever,* would be the best thing for her. Oh dear, what would Winston think if he knew how her emotions were stirring? Here, after three years with a man she had professed to love, she was pining for someone new?

No, not new. Someone *else.*

Someone with a fiancée.

"However," the announcer continued, "the band will carry on with Terence Knowles, the band's piano player and manager. He will take over for Detective Belmonte tonight."

A half-hearted round of applause rose from the crowd as the tuxedo-clad musicians bravely jumped into a rendition of "Ain't that a Shame". Mr. Knowles' singing was adequate, but obviously lacked the strong voice of a lead singer. About a dozen young people jumped up and danced in front of the stage, and the crowd seemed to settle in and enjoy the entertainment despite themselves.

"I much prefer Miguel's voice," Gloria remarked. "He reminds me of Elvis Presley or Carl Perkins."

For Rosa's part, she continued to embrace the news. Instead of an evening of conflicting emotions, she could now just have a drink and enjoy herself. She recognized Raul Mendez, the accountant for the California Polio Research Foundation, playing bass guitar for the band. He looked unsteady, and Rosa wondered if he had been drinking. Her suspicion was confirmed when, after playing a thirty-minute set, he wandered over to them during the break carrying a drink in his right hand and a cigarette in his left.

"Well, well, well," Mr. Mendez said without introduction. "Nice to see you young ladies again, ya know? Can I sit here? I only have ten minutes, so I promise not to bore you too much." He loosened his bow tie, pushed his half-rimmed glasses up on his nose, and without waiting for an answer, sat down next to Rosa on the padded bench seat. He pulled out a red and white pack of cigarettes and offered it to the ladies. "*Delicados* brand. I buy them in Mexico. Much cheaper, ya know? Menthol helps freshen the breath."

It wasn't working, Rosa thought as she leaned back and declined.

"I know what you're th-th-inking. That I've had too much." He grinned boyishly as he lifted the near-empty glass into the air. "I don't usually, but I'm afraid the free tequila that was offered to the band was too tempting." He chuckled dryly, and the smile quickly faded.

"Do you know why Detective Belmonte was called away at such short notice?" Rosa asked. Even though she now refused to think of Miguel, the man, she couldn't stop thinking about the case. Perhaps Aunt Louisa was right that Rosa wasn't happy unless she had a big puzzle to solve.

"It's not like he confides in me," Mr. Mendez slurred. "Not a big man like De-detective *Bel-elmonte*. I'm not good enough for the likes of him. But I'm pretty sure it's because of that broad who bit the dust last night."

"I wonder if they got the results back from the pathologist," Rosa said. Tests usually took time, but Santa Bonita was a small town. The labs here were probably slower than most.

Gloria shrugged. "That could be."

"If foul play was indicated in the postmortem, the investigation would kick into high gear. There'd likely be a shuffling of personnel at the police department to ensure enough officers were assigned to the case."

"Whoa!" Raul Mendez regarded Rosa with tequila-glazed eyes. "You seem to know a lot about that."

"Rosa is also a police officer," Gloria said proudly. "In London."

Raul Mendez blinked slowly and said, "Oh." He seemed confused and opened his mouth to say more but seemed to think better of it.

"Who on earth would want harm to come to poor Florence Adams?" Gloria asked.

"Well, if you ask me. . ." Raul leaned forward, his voice taking on a conspiratorial tone, "I think Shirley Philpott did it."

Rosa stared back in shock. "The Chief Medical Examiner's wife?"

"Exactly." Mr. Mendez nodded his head one time more than necessary.

"That seems hard to believe." Gloria sounded aghast. "She's such a nice lady and very devoted to the charity. What does she have against Florence Adams that would make her want to kill her?"

"What always brings the worst out in people?" Mr. Mendez sneered as he pushed up on his glasses. "Money, ya know, that's what."

"I don't understand," Rosa said. "Does Shirley Philpott have financial troubles?"

"Well, . . ." Raul Mendez seemed to forget his earlier distrust of Rosa. "You know that Florence Adams and Shirley Philpott are cousins, right? Just happens there's a wealthy uncle in the picture who owns two huge estates in Palos Verdes. William Lawrence is the man's name."

He leaned in to whisper in Rosa's ear. "I happen to be the bookkeeper for that account. I can tell you this; William Lawrence is an exceedingly wealthy man who made his money in California real estate. He is now eighty-six years old and very ill. He has no children of his own, his wife died ten years ago, and the only real heirs are his two nieces."

Rosa doubted that Mr. Lawrence would be impressed by Mr. Mendez's loose lips, but was happy to have been given the information. Mr. Mendez attempted to straighten, lost his balance, but saved himself by grabbing on to the table. As if he hadn't just fallen over in front of a group of strangers, he continued, more loudly than was called for. "It is well known to acquaintances of the cousins that Florence Adams was Mr. Lawrence's favorite because Shirley married Melvin Philpott." He stabbed the air with his finger as if to make a stronger point. "And he doesn't like Philpott."

"What does he have against the medical examiner?" Rosa asked.

"Gettin' to that." Raul Mendez belched into his hand, and Rosa and Gloria shared a grimace.

"When William Lawrence's wife died, he was convinced it was murder. God only knows why. He's a bit of an odd old codger. Philpott ruled it death by suicide. Well, the old man was in incen . . . incens . . . furious! He thought the ruling brought shame to his marriage and be*eee*smirched his reputation, not to mention that suicide canceled any benefits from life insurance. Anyway, he railed against the police for months, ya know, wrote to the editor of the local paper, and sent Philpott nasty letters."

As if in slow motion, Mr. Mendez checked his wristwatch. "Anyways, rumor has it that he made Florence Adams the main beneficiary of his estate. She would get eighty-five percent of all his assets, with the other fifteen going to Shirley. I gotta go."

"Wait," Rosa said. "How do you know all of this?"

He stared back with a sloppy grin and glassy eyes. "Lovely Flo and I once dated. A long, long time ago, still in high school. She liked her rum and cokes already back then, and apparently I was a *big drunken mistake*." He fiddled with his lips and chuckled. "I'm not the only one who talks too much when I've been drinking." Mr. Mendez pushed up his glasses, smiled wanly, and after almost stumbling over an empty chair, wandered over to the stage.

"That's very interesting," Gloria mused. "But still . . . it seems a rather weak motive for murdering your cousin."

"Perhaps," Rosa said. Anyone in police work knew

that people killed for less. "There could be a provision in the will stating if Florence Adams dies first, Shirley Philpott becomes the sole beneficiary. That's a lot of money and some prime real estate."

And an excellent motive for murder.

7

*W*hen Rosa and Gloria returned to the Forrester mansion, they were surprised to find Aunt Louisa still awake. Perched on the aqua-blue section couch in the living room, a glass of sherry in hand, Louisa set her drink on the glass-topped coffee table that sat in the center of a yellow area rug.

"The police have officially declared this case a suspicious death," she said simply when Rosa and Gloria walked in. "Shirley Philpott is being held for questioning."

"How did you find out?" Gloria plopped into a matching, slender Scandinavian-style chair.

"I spoke to the mayor and demanded to know if Dr. Rayburn, the acting pathologist, had submitted a report yet."

Rosa expected that an absence of seawater in Miss Adams' lungs had been confirmed, which would rule out accidental drowning. It could explain why Mrs. Philpott had been in such a hurry earlier that day. She might've heard her husband's suspicions and figured she'd be picked up by the police for questioning.

Rosa lowered herself onto the opposite end of the couch. "And the cause of death?"

"Not determined, only that drowning has been officially ruled out." Aunt Louisa crossed her legs dramatically. "I have no idea why they suspect Shirley Philpott. The idea is absurd! The police are off on the wrong trail, just like I thought they would be." She looked directly at Rosa, "I hope you'll consider what we talked about earlier. In my opinion, you're the better choice."

Rosa suddenly felt bone-weary and would much rather have gone to bed than continue this conversation.

"The police must have their reasons for suspecting Mrs. Philpott, Aunt Louisa. Perhaps it's better to let Detective Belmonte do his job."

Gloria squinted, her eyes moving from Rosa to her mother and back again. "What are you both talking about?"

Lips pinching as if she was rather put out at the question, Aunt Louisa cast a glance at her daughter.

She must've decided that Gloria wouldn't stay out of the conversation anyway, so gave her a straight answer.

"I want Rosa involved in this case. Someone with her background and training could help get the police on track instead of their wild goose chases that will cause dissension and ill will all over this town."

Gloria tilted her head. "But Rosa's a visitor."

"She's also unbiased," Aunt Louisa said. "You know how entwined small towns can be, everyone covering for the other. Rosa's our best chance of getting to the truth."

Rosa couldn't help but feel flattered and a little unnerved by her aunt's high expectations of her. She did not, however, like being talked about like she wasn't in the room.

"I'm rather unfamiliar with how things are done in America," Rosa protested.

"Oh, nonsense. You lived here for years. It's like riding a bike. Before you know it, you'll forget you even left." There was a sparkle of mirth in Aunt Louisa's eyes, but also a challenge.

Would Rosa back down or accept?

Grandma Sally shuffled into the room and sat upright in one of the chairs.

"What are you still doing up?" Aunt Louisa said.

"I'm not so old that I fall asleep right after dinner. I heard you chattering."

Aunt Louisa scoffed. "You're afraid of missing out on the gossip."

Grandma Sally didn't deny it. Instead, she looked at Rosa. "I'm afraid I have to agree with Louisa on this one, Rosa. There's no way that Shirley Philpott murdered her cousin Florence. I think you should get involved."

"But she's on vacation!" Gloria complained. "And besides, she just can't go headlong into a police investigation without authorization."

Although thankful that Gloria was sticking up for her, Rosa knew her Aunt Louisa was an influential woman who wouldn't give up once she decided she wanted something.

"Mayor Phillips is in total agreement that Rosa should be invited into this case to help the Santa Bonita Police Department—especially after I explained Rosa's credentials and that she had more experience in murder cases than Officer Belmonte."

Rosa's scalp prickled with humiliation. "You didn't say that! Aunt Louisa! I'll be hated and despised by every member of the force! And it's *Detective* Belmonte!" Rosa could only imagine what Miguel would think of her now.

Not that she cared.

That much.

Aunt Louisa didn't seem troubled by Rosa's

outburst. "Didn't you just solve a murder case in London?"

Before her wedding, Rosa had been part of an investigative team in an open-and-shut case. However, it was the cases she hadn't solved that stayed with her, and there was one investigation in particular that often kept her awake at night.

Vivien Eveleigh, Rosa's close childhood friend, had been murdered in 1951, and despite the combined talents of Rosa's parents and other skilled members of Scotland Yard, the trail had gone cold.

Vivien's death had left Rosa emotionally traumatized and had propelled her into Vivien's brother Winston's vortex. A romance birthed in crisis.

As Aunt Louisa's guest, Rosa could hardly defy her. "I want to go on record as saying that I protest at being coerced into this investigation." She glared back at her Aunt Louisa, who appeared to regard Rosa with a surprised expression.

Louisa's mouth formed a tight line.

Rosa leaned toward her aunt. "I came here intending to have a break from what has been a very stressful time. Frankly, Aunt Louisa, I'm disappointed that you talked to the mayor without my consent. Please don't do anything like that again." She paused there to let that sink in.

The silence in the room roared like a freight train.

Apparently, the three Hartigan women weren't used to someone addressing Louisa Forrester in this manner.

"Now," Rosa began again slowly, "I do realize the gravity of this situation, so I will offer this: I'll talk to Detective Belmonte tomorrow morning. I'm sure he will have heard from the mayor by then." She shot her Aunt Louisa another disapproving look. "If I sense any hesitancy, any reticence at the prospect of my working with the police on this case, I will not even entertain the thought any further. Is that clear?"

It took a moment for her aunt to respond. Finally, the corner of her mouth raised in a slight smile, and her eyes brightened with respect. "You are truly your mother's daughter, young lady."

*a*s a concession, Aunt Louisa offered Rosa unlimited use of the Bel Air. Having first learned to drive in America, Rosa found that switching her reflexes to the right-hand side was, as Aunt Louisa liked to say, like riding a bike.

She parked across from the Santa Bonita Police Department and took a moment to fortify herself, still not believing what she'd agreed to do, and quite certain she was about to make a fool of herself.

The police station in Santa Bonita looked nothing like Scotland Yard, the metropolitan police headquarters in London. A much smaller, Spanish mission-style building, with a red clay-tile roof and white stucco exterior, had a cement walkway lined with palm trees that swayed in the warm breeze. The pleasant setting contrasted with the impending doom she felt as she walked to the front door.

She took a deep, calming breath of the jasmine-scented air, opened the glass door and stepped inside. The plump middle-aged lady at reception glanced up. "Can I help you?"

"I'm Rosa Reed and am here to see Detective Belmonte. I called earlier to arrange an appointment."

"Yes, he did mention he was expecting you."

The woman led Rosa down a hall and through a large room containing several cubicles where officers were tapping on typewriters, rustling papers, or talking on the telephone. It was a scene very familiar to Rosa.

Miguel had a private office partitioned from the rest of the officer stations by a frosted-glass wall and a wood-veneer door which was opened wide. Through it, she saw him at his desk talking on the telephone. Seeing him for the first time in a shirt and tie in his position of detective made her breath catch in her throat. The last time she remembered feeling this sensation was when she'd first laid eyes on him in his soldier's uniform.

Winston had never had that effect on her. Poor Winston. Still, Rosa was sure she'd done the right thing by not marrying him. Her only regret was that it had taken too long for her to realize that he wasn't the man for her.

Miguel stilled when he spotted her, his eyes lingering for a moment. A smile came a second too late as he gestured for her to take a seat in the chair across from his desk.

Like most detectives' offices, this one was austere and efficient. Blinds on the window were closed against the mid-morning sun. Several metal filing cabinets lined the wall, and above Miguel's desk hung a framed diploma from the Los Angeles Police Academy. Rosa idly looked for a picture of his fiancée, but Miguel didn't have personal objects in view.

"Sorry about that," he said as he hung up the phone. He walked out from behind his desk.

"Don't apologize," Rosa replied. "I'm grateful you made time to see me at such short notice. I know you're busy right now."

"Yes, I am, but it's nice to see you. Besides, it's not often we get a visit from a foreign dignitary here at the Santa Bonita Police Department."

"Well, I'm not exactly the Queen, but I am quite famous, you know." Rosa adopted a mock posh accent while batting her eyelashes and pretending to fluff the back of her hair with her left hand. "Well, at least my Aunt Louisa thinks so," she quipped, which caused him to laugh.

Why did he have to be so blasted easy to talk to? Rosa wished they could just have a pleasant social visit over drinks and dinner with an easy, satisfying conversation. Instead, she had to broach a subject she was loathe to get into. Might as well jump right in.

"Miguel, I'm sorry about that phone call you got from the mayor's office today."

"It was actually Police Chief John Delvecchio who received the call. But yes, I know all about it."

"Of course, well . . . as you know, my aunt can be quite obstinate and sometimes loses sight of propriety."

"Your aunt is an interesting woman."

"And very persuasive. I want you to know that I had nothing to do with that, and I'm not keen to join any investigation whatsoever. I know that the case has now been labeled as suspicious, and that you and your team are more than capable of solving it. I'm afraid I would probably just get in the way."

"Oh, I doubt that very much."

Rosa blinked back her surprise. She'd expected him to agree. In case he'd missed her point, she pressed on. "Furthermore, I am here on holiday, of sorts." Rosa shrugged her shoulders and shook her head.

Miguel cocked his head as he leaned casually against his desk. "Of sorts?"

"Yes, of sorts." There was no way on God's green earth she would ever tell him the real reason she'd come to California. "How am I going to relax and be

79

part of a murder investigation at the same time? Honestly, I don't know what my aunt was thinking."

Rosa was determined to make it easy for Miguel to reject her. Then she could go back to Aunt Louisa and say she'd tried but had been dismissed.

"I want you on this case. The chief agrees with me."

Rosa stared back, stunned. "What?"

"It's up to you, of course. You have to decide what you want to do on your holiday-of-sorts. But for my part, I want this case solved quickly and accurately, and I'd be a fool to dismiss your offer to assist. Your reputation at Scotland Yard is stellar. Yes, we called."

"Oh," was all Rosa could say.

"We have a suspect being held, but there are many questions still unanswered." Miguel rubbed the back of his neck. "This is a relatively small town, Rosa. Now, I've never been to England, but I know they drive on the wrong side of the road—"

"The *other* side of the road," Rosa interjected. "Not the wrong side."

Miguel's lips twitched, and Rosa caught a glimpse of a dratted dimple.

"Yes, right, and, for reasons unfathomable to me, they eat a lot of something called steak and kidney pie. But I'm afraid that's where my knowledge ends. Experience has taught me, in towns like Santa Bonita, people tend to feed on their own drama. Help from someone with an objective perspective like you would be appreciated." He folded his arms as though waiting for her response.

Rosa was speechless. Not only was his response to Aunt Louisa's intrusion unexpected, but also, she felt a disconcerting bubble of pleasure. The thought of working with Miguel tickled her belly. She stared back at him. "I hate steak and kidney pie."

Those adorable dimples made a full-on appearance. "Anyone with any sense would."

Rosa grinned back. "However, the Queen likes it. And she is quite sensible. She always wears sensible shoes."

Miguel chuckled. "I bet if my mother cooked her an enchilada, the Queen of England would never look at steak and kidney pie again. No matter her footwear."

"That could be true," Rosa returned, "but she'd still drive on the left side. Even a good enchilada wouldn't change that."

Miguel nodded solemnly. "Other things, but not that."

Rosa had missed their cheeky back-and-forth banter. After all these years, the chemistry between them still flourished. It was reminiscent of the conversations her mother and father often had while discussing the day's events over a glass of brandy at

Hartigan House. As a teenager, Rosa had sometimes listened in on and even participated in those discussions, which often turned comedic. Witticism was a way to offset the seriousness of the cases they were involved in.

Rosa realized suddenly, *this* was what had been missing with Winston. She felt happy yet profoundly sad.

Locking eyes with Miguel, she said, "Are you sure you want me on this case?"

Miguel's demeanor changed. He wasn't joking anymore. "Absolutely."

9

*R*osa thought for a moment and then said, "All right, if you're sure. It is terribly magnanimous of you to allow an outsider to join you on the case. Many detectives would be threatened by that."

"I've seen too much to be threatened, and life is complicated enough without harboring petty insecurities." Miguel walked around his desk and lowered himself into his rolling office chair. "Honestly, I think Chief Delvechio was all too happy at the prospect of having you onboard for this case. We've had some budget cuts recently, and we're short on manpower."

"I see." Rosa nodded playfully. "So, it's more of a financial decision than a matter of my competence."

Miguel grinned. "Well, not as far as I'm concerned,

83

but you'll have to take that up with the boss. Can you start right now?"

"I suppose I can." She opened her purse to take out a notepad, but then realized she didn't have one with her.

"I have extras." Miguel seemed to know what she was searching for. He reached into his desk and pulled out a new pocket-sized police notebook and handed it to her. "You'll need your own pen. When it comes to my pens, I am very territorial."

"No problem." Rosa proudly held up her favorite black Paper Mate Deluxe ballpoint pen.

"If this was a Rory Calhoun Western movie," Miguel added with a chuckle, "I'd deputize you and give you a large silver badge."

"Not necessary. A notepad will do."

"All right, then." Miguel pushed his chair away from his desk and stood. "You're now officially on this case as a special consultant to the Santa Bonita Police Department. Welcome." He reached for his straw fedora and placed it on his head. "Now, let's go."

"What? Wait. Where are we going?" Rosa closed her handbag and got to her feet.

"As nice as it would be to sit and chat over tea and biscuits like I hear you do in London, we have a case to solve. I'm just about to head over to the morgue to talk to Dr. Rayburn. You'll come?"

"Of course."

They left the rear exit of the building, and Miguel strode to a police cruiser. With white doors, black rounded hood, large circular headlights, and short black tail fins, it was a sharp contrast to its British white and powder-blue counterpart. Rosa recognized the car as the famous "police package" made by the Ford Motor Company. The cars were the envy of the Metropolitan Police Force who had nothing like them. The American police cruisers boasted specialized, more powerful engines, precise handling suspension, and much larger space in the boot or the "trunk" as the Americans called it—perfect for accommodating the bulky radio equipment.

Rosa slid into the passenger side of the car, and Miguel pulled out of the lot and onto the street.

"I know you have Shirley Philpott in for questioning," Rosa said, diving right in with a few questions of her own. "So, I assume she's your prime suspect. On what grounds?"

Miguel turned inland off the main road. A band of impressive mountains framed the horizon, and Rosa remembered how much she'd missed seeing them.

"She was actually released an hour ago," Miguel replied. "We didn't have enough to charge her. Yet."

"Did she tell you what she and her cousin argued about?"

Miguel stopped at a traffic light. "She says Miss Adams was upset because she overheard some charity contributors talking about her role in the charity. That she didn't do enough to deserve the financial draw she was taking as one of the administrators. Mrs. Philpott claims she was trying to calm her down."

Miguel paused to let Rosa catch up on writing notes, then continued. "We have an eyewitness who saw Florence Adams walking out onto the wharf, drink in hand, apparently looking somewhat inebriated at roughly fifteen minutes after seven. Shirley Philpott was seen by another witness walking out onto the pier five minutes later. That's twenty minutes before the body was found, which makes Shirley Philpott the last person to have seen Miss Adams alive."

They'd reached the local hospital, a one-story, white stucco complex, and Miguel pulled into one of the parking spots. "At that time of day, the sun would be down, and it would've been nearly impossible to see the end of the pier from the beach. So, no-one actually saw Miss Adams' fall."

"What does Shirley Philpott say about walking out on the wharf?" Rosa asked.

"She says she went out to see how Miss Adams was doing and claims she was drunk and inconsolable, so Shirley came back to the party. However, we've got no witnesses who can confirm any part of this event."

"Most people were enjoying your Sinatra performance during that time."

"Yes, that's true," Miguel said with a subtle smile. "One day, I'll have to thank Mr. Sinatra for those great songs."

They exited the police cruiser, and Rosa followed Miguel to the hospital entrance. "Have you determined a motive for Mrs. Philpott?"

"That's a bit of a complicated story." Miguel opened the glass door and allowed Rosa to step ahead. The lobby acted as a waiting room with chairs lining the walls and well-worn speckled linoleum on the floor. Miguel guided her down a corridor towards the back of the building.

"Let me guess," Rosa said quietly once they were out of earshot of bustling nurses and shuffling patients. "It involves a rich uncle who doesn't like Melvin Philpott because of a ruling on a suicide case."

Miguel came to a stop and stared down at her with a look of astonishment. "How did you know that?"

Rosa smirked and continued. "There's also a will involved, along with the fact that Shirley Philpott could now be the sole beneficiary of a large amount of wealth due to Florence Adams's death."

"If you have a crystal ball, then yes, I *am* threatened by you joining this case. That's an unfair advantage! Santa Bonita Police Department might have a budget for one session with a tarot card reader, maybe, but not for a crystal ball. Those things aren't cheap!"

Rosa laughed. "No crystal ball. Just a slightly drunk, near-sighted bass player."

"Aha," Miguel thought for a moment, then continued walking. "The gig at the American Legion last night. Mr. Mendez had one too many."

"Nicely done, Mr. Holmes."

"Raul does the accounting for William Lawrence, so that's how he found out about all that. He brought it to my attention. I guess I should've told him to keep the information to himself."

Rosa understood. It was human nature to share gossip. "Okay, so we have motive and opportunity, but no means yet. Is that correct? Since Miss Adams didn't drown, it means Mrs. Philpott didn't push her off the pier."

"We are hoping test results from the lab will point to means," Miguel replied.

"Shirley Philpott is the Chief Medical Examiner's wife. I'm guessing you haven't let the media know about this?" Rosa tapped her notebook with her pen.

"No, not yet. I'm hoping to avoid the press for now, but I have already received several phone calls from local papers. They've all gotten the standard comments from me about it being too soon for details on the inves-tigation."

"Have you found out who the mystery man is that I saw arguing with the victim at the foot of the stairs on the beach? He seemed very suspicious."

They reached a set of steel doors with a sign on one of them that read "MORGUE".

"He's a person of interest that we are looking for," Miguel said. "No sign of him yet."

The first thing Rosa saw as they entered the Santa Bonita City Morgue was a sterile waiting room and two glass-walled offices. A nameplate on one was inscribed *Chief Medical Examiner, Dr. Melvin Philpott*, and the other *Dr. Larry Rayburn, Assistant Medical Examiner*.

A pretty nurse approached and smiled. "Hello, Detective."

"I'm looking for Dr. Rayburn."

"I'm afraid he's stepped out for a moment. Would you like to make an appointment?"

"Just let him know I've dropped by."

Miguel let the door close behind them as they stepped back into the corridor. "Forgive me for not introducing you. She's an intern, and I'd rather keep certain things close to my chest for now."

Rosa understood. She was disappointed that the pathologist was unavailable but that didn't keep her mind from dwelling on the case. She glanced down at her notebook and with a grimace brought up the next notation. "What do you know about Vanessa Forrester?"

"The woman who found the body? Yes, I questioned her at the beach. She was quite distraught, but she claims to have seen nothing, and we have no reason to doubt that."

"You're probably aware that she was once married to my cousin, Clarence."

Miguel caught her gaze and nodded. "And she's the former daughter-in-law of your Aunt Louisa, who insisted you be brought on to this case."

Rosa tapped her lips with her pen. "A rather interesting coincidence."

"Agreed."

"Wouldn't that make my involvement in the case a conflict of interest?"

Miguel paused, his palm on the door of the exterior door, ready to push. "At the moment, neither your aunt nor your cousin are persons of interest."

"I wouldn't be so sure about that," Rosa said.

Miguel narrowed his gaze. "What do you mean?"

Rosa hesitated. If she was going to work this case with Miguel, she had to share every bit of information she knew, even if it came back to haunt her. The night before, at the Legion, Raul Mendez hadn't been the only one to have one too many. Gloria had gotten a little too happy herself. Rosa didn't know if her cousin remembered what she'd said, but Rosa hadn't forgotten how shocked she'd felt at hearing the news.

"What is it, Rosa?" Miguel prompted.

"My cousin Clarence and Florence Adams once dated."

10

*R*osa followed Clarence as he drove the 1955 bright-red Ford Fairlane, a recent addition to the Forresters' fleet of cars, into the sizeable six-car garage. Easing out of the driver's seat, Clarence tugged on the lapels of his shiny slate-blue suit jacket and straightened his narrow black tie then narrowed his eyes at Rosa.

Rosa put the car into park and turned off the ignition, cutting the song *Rockin' Robin* out mid-chorus. She did a double-take when her gaze landed on the 1941 Schwinn Deluxe Hollywood bicycle parked in the corner. Rosa could see it had been kept shining clean. A wire basket was fastened to the front fender and handlebars, and a small ringer sat on the left hand-grip. A chromium finish sparkled on the rims. Rosa loved this bike. When she was fifteen, too young to drive a car, the Schwinn had become a symbol of personal freedom. She'd often ridden it down the main street or to the beach.

Rosa exited the Bel Air and carefully closed the door.

"Howdy, detective," Clarence said.

Rosa didn't miss the hint of sarcasm in his voice. "Hi, Clarence."

"Solved the case already?"

"No, but I do have a few questions."

He patted the hood of his car with affection. "About the Fairlane?"

Rosa shook her head. It would surprise her cousin to know that, despite her pretty clothes, she was rather well acquainted with car engines. Her mother had insisted that she'd learned the basics, and as a police officer, the information had come in handy more than once.

She smoothed her skirt—navy blue with white polka dots—and pulled off her short white summer gloves. "Actually, I understand that you and the deceased were acquainted."

"The deceased?"

"Yes. Miss Adams."

"Oh." He shrugged. "She was fairly well known around town, and she worked with my mother, so sure. We were acquainted."

Rosa stared at her cousin with disapproval. "I think you know what I'm getting at, Clarence. Is it true that you and Florence Adams were once romantically involved?"

Clarence folded his arms across his chest. "So, what if we were?"

"Did the affair happen while you were married to Vanessa?"

"What does that have to do with anything?"

"You and Vanessa were both at the scene of the crime at high tide. Vanessa *found* the body."

"What, wait—are you suggesting that Vanessa killed Flo?"

"It's motive."

"That's crazy."

"Did you end things with Florence?"

"I had to. She wanted to get married. I wasn't about to jump from the frying pan to the fire."

"I bet Florence didn't like that."

"She was hysterical. I told Mom to stop working with her. She was bad for business, bad for our family name."

Obviously, Aunt Louisa hadn't agreed, since Florence hadn't been fired.

Rosa ducked her chin. "You know that looks bad for you, don't you?"

Clarence seared her with a look. "Are you accusing

me now?"

"I'm not," Rosa was quick to say. The last thing she wanted was to get on Clarence's wrong side. "But don't be surprised if Detective Belmonte eventually asks to speak to you. I just thought I should warn you."

Rosa found Gloria reading leisurely at the pool. The sun shone brightly, and a warm breeze caused the palms to flutter. A yellow finch daintily bathed itself in the cool waters of a cement fountain surrounded by a garden of red and yellow roses.

Gloria glanced up, and with her gold-framed, green-lens sunglasses and wide-brimmed hat, she looked every bit the TV star she aspired to be.

Upon seeing Rosa, she raised the LOOK magazine in her lap to show off the cover. The subtitles read *Segregation in the North*, and *Music or Madness: The Rock & Roll Ruckus*. Below those was a head and shoulders shot of Elizabeth Taylor, her rich, dark curls blowing softly in the breeze.

"Isn't she the most beautiful woman you've ever seen?" Gloria asked.

"Gorgeous," Rosa admitted. The violet eyed beauty with her trademark dark brows was known around the globe.

Gloria patted her own light brunette waves.

"Maybe I should go darker. Or I could go blond? Platinum like Marilyn Monroe?"

"Don't be silly," Rosa said. "Your hair is lovely."

"Oh, I suppose it's good enough for now." Gloria pushed off her lounger and languidly moved to a chair at the patio table. "Come, join me. Señora Gomez has made me a delightful lunch, far too much for one person."

Rosa sat across from Gloria, and her stomach growled at the sight of tuna and cucumber sandwiches. She was instantly reminded of home. Such finger food was very English, especially with tea. Of course, in England, the drink was hot. A pitcher of iced tea and a single half-filled glass sat on a table nearby.

Gloria waved at the pool boy, "Ricardo! Be a dear and get a glass for Miss Reed."

"I can go myself, you know," Rosa said, feeling a tad embarrassed.

"Phew," Gloria said with a casual wave. "I need you to tell me all about your adventures. I'm bored silly. All my good friends are off on fantastic summer vacations." Her well-manicured eyebrows arched playfully. "Did you see the handsome detective?"

Rosa felt herself blush. "It's hot out already, isn't it?" She fanned herself with her hand. The month of June in London was a lot cooler. "I'm not used to all of this sunshine."

"Don't change the subject, sweetheart."

"Well, if you must know, I did. Aunt Louisa was quite insistent that I help with this case, and Detective Belmonte agreed."

"Oh, lucky you!"

Ricardo returned with Rosa's glass and poured for her. She sincerely thanked him, then immediately took a drink.

"Come on," Gloria whined. "Won't you tell me anything?"

Rosa patted her lips with a linen napkin. "Were Clarence and Vanessa very much in love?"

"Oh." Gloria's expression darkened. "That's out of the blue."

"I met Vanessa for the first time after she found the body, so naturally, I'm curious. I wasn't here to witness the romance."

"I suppose, but—" Gloria leaned in to whisper, even though no one, not even Ricardo, was about. "They *had* to get married."

It was Rosa's turn to release a soft "Oh."

"Mom was furious, of course. Called Vanessa terrible names and accused her of chasing family money. There was no stopping—things—once they were started, and Mom finally decided that Clarence deserved whatever it was that was coming to him."

Rosa twisted her lips to one side as she pondered

this information. "I don't know if you remember this," she began, "but you told me that Clarence and Florence Adams were once involved."

Gloria blushed. "Starting immediately, I'm swearing off tequila."

"Did the affair happen during the marriage?"

"Yes, and afterwards too."

"I imagine there was bad blood between the ladies."

"You can say that again," Gloria said. "It was a catfight whenever the two of them were in the same room."

"And you don't think it odd that Vanessa found Florence's body?"

Gloria cupped her mouth with her hand. "I thought it was a horrible coincidence. You don't think—"

"I'm just asking questions."

"You know, I shouldn't say this about my niece's mother, but Vanessa has a terrible temper."

Rosa selected another sandwich triangle. Had Vanessa Forrester been angry enough to kill?

eeling nostalgic, Rosa asked Aunt Louisa if she could take the Schwinn bicycle for a spin.

Aunt Louisa lowered the newspaper she'd been reading and stared at her over her reading glass. "Don't be silly. Take a car."

"I'd really rather ride the bicycle."

"Then go ahead. You don't have to ask every time you want to use something. *Mi casa es su casa.* Besides, wasn't that your bike anyways?"

"Yes, I guess so. Someone kept it clean and oiled, so I thought maybe someone had claimed it.

"We have someone on staff who keeps everything in the garage clean. It's still yours, if you want it."

After changing into a pair of teal-blue capri pants and a striped shirt, Rosa wheeled the Schwinn out onto the street and was soon happily pedaling her way through the affluent neighborhoods surrounding the Forrester mansion. The warm breeze teased her skin, and she felt grateful for a chance to clear her head.

As her mind swirled with facts and questions about the case, she cruised down the gentle slope towards the town. She was used to letting her mind go, almost subconsciously rehashing elements of a case she was working on, even while she was off duty having dinner or doing such things as watching a film. It was part of the territory of being a detective; one's mind was continually working. The first questions always came back to means, motive, and opportunity.

Who had the means to pull off a murder? That depended on the cause of death yet to be determined. Who stood to gain the most by the death of the victim? Unknown. Who had the opportunity to kill Florence Adams? Pretty much everyone who attended the polio charity event, though one could narrow it down to those who were known to have ventured away from the party. So far, the police had only done a thorough questioning of Shirley Philpott, but Rosa knew there would be more suspects forthcoming as the investigation kicked into a higher gear.

Hearing a vehicle come up behind her, Rosa directed the bike to the side of the road. Expecting the car to pass, she nearly jumped out of her skin when a siren blasted. She jolted to a stop and grabbed her heart.

Miguel!

A police cruiser parked right behind her, and Miguel, with his deep dimples, laughed. He stepped out of the car.

"You scared me half to death!"

"I'm sorry. I shouldn't have done that."

Rosa's pulse slowed, and she saw the humor. She would've done the same thing in his shoes. She bit her lip to keep from smiling. Miguel didn't have to know she'd already forgiven him.

"I had a flashback to the past," he said. "Are you sure it's not 1945 again?"

He kidded her, but his words poked her heart. The ripping emotional pain she'd attached to that time obviously hadn't stayed with him. She forced a smile.

"I was just on my way to the station," Rosa said.

"How fortunate I came by. I'm on my way to the morgue. Apparently, Dr. Rayburn has returned. Do you want to come?"

"Yes."

Miguel opened the trunk. "I'll give you a ride."

Rosa watched as Miguel effortlessly lifted her bike and secured it in the trunk of the cruiser, then she opened the car door to get in.

Miguel's dark brow jumped. "Are you driving?"

"Oh, sorry, wrong side." Rosa blushed, quickly circled the car, and got in the other side. She chided herself for forgetting that American cars had the steering wheels on the left.

WEARING A WHITE DOCTOR'S SMOCK, a blue-eyed man in his thirties emerged from the second office behind the glass at the morgue. Rosa blinked in surprise, both at the doctor's youth and his alarming good looks. She for one, preferred her attending physicians to be older and on the homely side, and she was pretty sure she'd feel the same way if she were dead!

She kept her expression cool and professional.

Miguel made introductions. "This is Rosa Reed. She's an officer with the London Metropolitan Police and will be helping us on this investigation as a special consultant."

Dr. Rayburn held her gaze, then he shifted a clipboard to his left hand and extended his right. "Larry Rayburn. It's a pleasure."

Rosa's lips twitched upward at Dr. Rayburn's Texan accent.

His gaze moved to Miguel. "Detective Belmonte." The young pathologist's interest returned to Rosa. "Aren't y'all part of the Forrester family?"

"A relative, yes. Louisa Forrester is my aunt."

"I see," Dr. Rayburn continued, "I've been assigned the Adams' case. I'm assuming that's why y'all are here?"

Miguel nodded. "Do you have anything new to report? Cause of death?"

"Kindly follow me."

At the end of a short corridor, they entered the autopsy room. The floor was smooth, white-painted cement. The walls, tiled white and yellow, produced an echoed acoustic like a small gymnasium. Stainless steel cupboards and countertops lined the walls and displayed various surgical instruments and jars of chemicals. Hanging from the ceiling, a large steel tray with a round scale meter above it measured the weight of organs and body parts. A strong smell of formalin antiseptic permeated the air, a scent Rosa was familiar with having made many trips to mortuaries in London.

In the center of the room, two bodies, covered in white cloth, lay on operating gurneys. Dr. Rayburn walked over to one and uncovered the head. Florence Adams' brown hair had dried now, and her bloodless face seemed almost placid. Dr. Rayburn also revealed her hands and arms.

"This is a bizarre case. Death wasn't a result of drowning as there was no seawater in the lungs. However, the body shows signs consistent with the cessation of life by asphyxiation. Lack of oxygen resulted in death."

"She was strangled?" Rosa asked.

"The obvious signs of strangulation are absent. No bruisin' on the neck, and the hyoid bone remains intact. Even if she was intoxicated and subsequently smothered, there are no defensive wounds anywhere on her body. However, there are vertical scratch marks on her neck and upper chest. The skin fragments and blood we found under her fingernails are her own. This means she wasn't passed out when she suffocated. She was conscious."

"What makes you think she suffocated?" Miguel asked.

"Signs of suffocation usually include very high levels of carbon dioxide in the blood and extremely bloodshot eyes." Dr. Rayburn opened one of the deceased's eyelids. The ordinarily white area of the eyeball was red with purple splotches. "What's baffling about this," the pathologist continued, "is that the symptoms are consistent with the inhalation of a pulmonary agent."

Rosa was stunned. "Poison gas?"

Dr. Rayburn nodded. "Phosgene comes to mind. It was used in the latter part of the First World War and was a more efficient killer than chlorine."

Rosa was impressed with Dr. Rayburn's knowledge

of what her parents had often referred to as the Great War. The events of the Second World War dominated the hearts and minds of most people nowadays.

"The esophagus was clamped almost completely shut." Dr. Rayburn walked over to a clipboard hanging from the end of the gurney and held it up. "The thing is, lab tests confirm that there isn't even a trace of anything like that in her blood. Besides, how can someone breathe in a poison gas standing at the end of a pier on the Pacific Ocean?"

Rosa was as perplexed as Dr. Rayburn. "What do the tests show?"

"High levels of carbon dioxide, which I already mentioned, is consistent with asphyxiation." He paused for a moment. "There are other interestin' things found in her in blood."

"Such as?" Miguel asked.

"The high level of alcohol indicates that she was drinkin' to excess on that evenin'. However, signs of ongoing alcoholism are absent, such as liver fibrosis, etcetera. Small traces of cocaine were also found. But . . ." He held up a finger. "The most surprisin' thing so far is that we found traces of digoxin, a drug used to treat cardiomyopathy."

"You mean she had a heart condition?" Rosa asked.

"Yes. More precisely, hypertrophic cardiomyopathy. She had abnormally thick heart muscles in her left ventricle. I called her doctor this morning, and he confirmed it. He was treating her and thought it to be under control. It's typically a genetic condition."

Miguel's eyebrows pulled together as he shook his head. "A person who has a heart condition should avoid things like alcohol and cocaine, shouldn't they?"

"Oh yeah," Dr. Rayburn nodded. "That's a dangerous mixture, not to mention if it's mixed with undue stress."

Rosa immediately thought of the two arguments she'd witnessed the night of Miss Adams's death.

"Despite all that," the doctor continued, "it wasn't the digoxin that killed her."

Miguel and Rosa shared a look.

"What did?" Miguel asked.

Dr. Rayburn worked his lips. "It appears that she inhaled a substance that mimics poison gas. Whatever it is, it must be very obscure. Whoever gave it to her probably hoped that because she fell into the water while drunk, and along with the fact that she was sniffing cocaine with a weak heart, that the true cause of death would be missed. I believe the killer wished to throw you off the scent."

He gave a pointed look at both Miguel and Rosa. "Florence Adams was most definitely murdered. We just don't know how yet."

12

*R*osa was stunned to find Gloria at the breakfast table the next morning, a coffee in one hand and a pen in the other. She circled something with a flourish then smiled when she saw Rosa approaching.

"Who's the early bird, now?" Gloria teased.

"I admit, I'm surprised to see you." Rosa pulled a chair from the table and took a seat.

Gloria's opened newspapers took up most of the table. "I've searched the want ads, but the only jobs available for women are secretarial or retail." She glanced at Rosa. "It's not like I need the money. I need *purpose.*"

"What happened to wanting to be a TV actress?"

"I considered what you said, and I'm not sure I'm ready to commit to something that requires going back to school. I thought I'd become a working girl and see how I like it."

Rosa bit the inside of her lip to keep from smirking. Most women who weren't married or mothers had no choice but to be working girls.

Señora Gomez had brought platters of fried eggs and bacon, fresh fruit, and a pitcher of freshly squeezed orange juice.

"I like clothes, flowers, and romance." Gloria's eyes brightened. "I know! I could be a wedding organizer! I hear it's becoming a real profession. Look at our garden. Imagine the beautiful bouquets I could create, and I've got a lot of ideas for wedding dresses. I've been to tons of weddings—"

Gloria stopped mid-sentence, her eyes growing wide with a glint of horror as they latched on to Rosa. Rosa couldn't stop the blush of embarrassment that crept up her neck. Her own wedding had been the last one the two had attended, and it had ended in humiliation.

"Oh, Rosa, I'm so insensitive!"

Rosa swallowed and forced a smile. "Nonsense. You'd make a terrific wedding organizer."

Gloria sighed. "It was just an idea. I'm honestly not sure what I want."

"What other kinds of things do you like to do?" Rosa asked.

Gloria wrinkled her nose. "I don't know. I like to dance. I'm actually taking ballroom dance classes. You should come sometime!"

Rosa did love to dance, and the offer was intriguing. But with her recent break up with Winston, and secretly, her confused feelings about Miguel, she just couldn't picture holding onto a strange man in such an intimate manner.

"We'll see," she said non-committedly. "At the moment, I'm busy with this task your mother assigned me to."

AFTER BREAKFAST, Rosa straddled the Schwinn and headed back into town. Now that she was on the case, it was natural that she'd pop into the police station occasionally.

It had nothing to do with wanting to see Miguel again.

Nothing at all.

It occurred to Rosa that her American counterparts might frown at her mode of transportation, but in London, riding one's bike was a common choice, even for the police.

The street leveled off, and she entered the outskirts of town and rode through a small industrial district with small factories, welding and steel fabrication shops, and several automotive repair businesses. She slowed the bike down as she entered the main street where the cafes and clothing stores were located. Stepping off the Schwinn, she walked a few blocks and admired the store window displays in the fashion shops. The smell of fresh pastry tempted her as she passed a bakery. A few minutes later, she emerged nibbling on a delicious custard-filled éclair while trying not to get any of it on her shirt. She grabbed her bike with her free hand and kept walking.

As Rosa rounded the side of the building, a soft mewling sound coming from behind a large metal garbage container piqued her curiosity. She leaned her bike against the building and walked towards the sound. Finding a dirty cardboard box on its side, she stooped to look inside. Two large, round green eyes peered back at her.

Oh, me bleedin' 'eart.

The eyes belonged to a tiny brown tabby huddled against the back of the box. Rosa scanned the area for the mother or the owner, but there was nothing to be found. Returning to the bakery, Rosa asked the lady at the counter if she knew anything about the kitten.

The clerk, a plump lady with a ready smile, stared back wide-eyed.

"A kitten, just left on its own?"

"It appears so."

"Oh, poor thing."

"You don't know anyone in the area who might've lost a kitten?" It was a pleasant way to ask if someone was hardhearted enough to leave a kitten to its own devices in a box in the alley.

"No, honey. No one in the building has said anything about a kitten or a cat."

Rosa bought another pastry for the woman's troubles. Just as she was about to step outside, a middle-aged woman wearing a simple day dress, hat and gloves, entered. Rosa's eye's widened in recognition.

"Mrs. Davidson?"

The lady's somber expression turned into a smile. "Rosa? Is it really you?"

"Yes, madam. I'm back for a visit." Rosa added a quick amendment. "Only just arrived. How's Nancy?"

Nancy Davidson had been Rosa's very best friend during their high school years. Sadly, they had lost touch over time.

"Nancy's married, as you might know. Eddie's a good enough fellow." The way she said it made Rosa doubt the woman's convictions. "All the girls are doing fine. My youngest, Marjorie's finding it hard to settle, but in time, I'm sure."

Nancy was the oldest of four girls. Marjorie was close in age to Gloria and they were good friends.

"Please let Nancy know I'm around," Rosa said. "I'd love to see her again."

"She's very busy with her three boys." Mrs. Davidson cocked her head. "You knew about them? I love them to pieces, but oh, they can be a handful."

Rosa smiled, though in truth she hadn't heard beyond the first one. "Please say hello for me."

"I will. You take care, honey."

Rosa had thought coming back to Santa Bonita would be like coming home, but in many ways it was like visiting the ghosts of one's past. She still couldn't face the library, which was a real shame. Rosa lived for the knowledge one could find in libraries. One's private collection could only go so far when it came to one's need to expand one's mind.

Shaking off the regrets of things she couldn't change, Rosa focused on her present company, the small abandoned brown tabby.

"Well 'ello, me ole mucker," Rosa said in a cockney accent. "Wot's the likes of you doin' out 'ere on yer own then, eh?"

It mewed again, and Rosa felt her heart melting like Julie's ice cream cone. She sighed and then reached in and gently grabbed the thin, trembling kitten. Cradling it in the crook of her arm, she guessed the little thing was about two months old. She checked under its tail to identify the gender.

"Hey, little boy, I'll bet you're hungry, aren't you?" She broke off a piece of her pastry, and the kitten eagerly licked the custard from Rosa's fingers with its tiny sandpaper tongue.

Now what? Rosa thought as she fed the kitten a few more pieces. She noticed a store on the street that sold kitchen and bath wares. While concealing the kitten, she purchased a cotton tea towel. Then, much to the amusement of the lady at the cash register, she carefully wrapped the kitten in the towel until just its tiny furry head was exposed. The kitten softly purred.

"What am I going to do with you?"

The kitten sleepily opened one eye, looked at her, and then closed it again.

Oh dear. Rosa's heart had just been ambushed. Rosa gently placed the kitten into her basket and mounted her bicycle. "I wonder how you're going to like England?" she said as she started toward the police station.

Miguel's eyes immediately fell on the sleeping kitten in Rosa's arms as she entered his office. "I've named him Diego," Rosa announced before Miguel had a chance to say anything.

"Interesting name. It's Spanish." He had a slight smirk on his face.

"I had some children's picture books that my parents bought me when I was a child. They were called *The Adventures of Deputy Diego*. He was a fearless and intelligent cat detective who solved many crimes in his Barcelona neighborhood. He was brown too." She kissed the tabby on the top of his head.

"Does this cat show any aptitude for police work?"

"He likes pastry."

"Well, that's a start." He nodded. "But I'm out of extra police notebooks," Miguel said simply. "Officer Diego will have to buy his own."

"I found him on my way here, and I couldn't just leave him beside a garbage bin."

"You know, in America, we have something called the SPCA."

"I know, I know. We have something like that in England too." Rosa looked at Miguel and pretended to pout. "Diego is destined for bigger things than the SPCA. I'll quickly run him home after our meeting."

"There's no time, he'll have to come with us." He grabbed the keys from the wall and motioned for Rosa to follow him.

"What? Where are we going?"

"To an address on Chambers Street. That's just down the beach from the pier where Miss Adams was killed."

"Have you found another witness?"

Miguel shook his head. His expression grew serious. "Not exactly. There's been another murder."

. . .

THE HOUSE on Chambers street was a small but well-kept ranch that overlooked the Pacific. Next to the house was a public stairway. Rosa recognized it as the same one she had witnessed a man trying to kiss Florence Adams, the same man who'd been watching Rosa when the body was found.

Two marked police cruisers were parked in the driveway, and an officer beside the front door snapped pictures of the house and yard. Rosa gently took Diego and placed the sleeping kitten on the seat beside her.

"It might get too hot in the car for the cat," Miguel cautioned. "This isn't London."

Rosa nodded, scooped up the kitten, and opened the door.

"Good morning," Miguel said to the man as they approached. "This is WPC Rosa Reed on loan to us from the London Metropolitan Police."

The officer with the camera, a middle-aged man in an ill-fitting uniform, stared at Rosa and then down at Diego with disregard. He refused to meet Rosa's eyes when she shook his hand.

"Where's the body?" Miguel said.

The officer pointed to the back of the house. "On the deck overlooking the beach. We just got here fifteen minutes ago and are still searching the place."

Rosa placed Diego on a padded chair in the living room. The kitten sneezed once, rubbed its paw over its nose, and then fell back asleep.

The house consisted of one bedroom just off the hallway, a bathroom, and a combined living room and dining room with an attached galley kitchen. A full bay window presented a spectacular view of the Pacific Ocean and the sandy beach that extended for miles on either side.

On the sundeck, two more officers stood over a prone figure on its back, clothed in khaki shorts, a green Hawaiian shirt, and a thin-knit cardigan partially torn off.

After making introductions, one of the officers handed rubber gloves to both Miguel and Rosa. "His name is Jason Brewster. We've been watching this guy for a while. Works as a chartered accountant, but we suspect he dealt cocaine to Santa Bonita's wealthier folk. An early morning jogger coming up those stairs from the beach spotted him through the rail."

Rose leaned over the body as she pulled on the gloves then glanced at Miguel. "This is the man I saw with Florence Adams on the night of her murder."

"You're sure?" Miguel asked.

"Quite. He had on the same shorts and sandals, only I think his Hawaiian shirt was blue."

Miguel bent down to examine the neck. "Same

scratch marks on the throat." He then picked up the man's left hand and pulled out a magnifying glass from a small kit he had brought along. "Blood traces. My guess—his own."

He handed the magnifying glass to Rosa, who examined the fingers and then nodded in confirmation. After gently prying open the mouth, she looked inside with the magnifier then checked the eyes—bloodshot. She glanced at Miguel. "Mystery asphyxiation."

Paying close attention to the exact route one would take from the sliding glass doors to where the body lay on the floor, Rosa studied the sundeck. Her father had taught her that a detective should notice every detail, no matter how small, when coming into a fresh crime scene. Anything out of place, a picture askew on the wall, an unfinished cup of coffee, or a note scribbled on a scrap of paper, you never knew what would tell the story.

Rosa returned to the living room and headed for the galley kitchen. Miguel followed her.

"He may have started choking here." Rosa pointed to the refrigerator door, not quite closed shut. "Then, walked, or rather stumbled past this sideboard, or buffet, as you call it." An embroidered runner balanced from the edge of the wooden sideboard as though a hand had haphazardly swiped at it. On the floor was a turned over plate with two broken chocolate cookies strewn beside it.

"He bumped against this lamp." Rosa glanced at a table lamp with the lampshade askew and then walked to the sliding glass doors. "Before going out on to the deck and collapsing . . . perhaps he intended to cry for help to anyone on the beach below."

Rosa noticed all the officers in the room had stopped to stare at her. Miguel had a slight smile on his lips.

"Well," she continued hesitantly, "this means if he was poisoned like Florence Adams was, it had a delayed reaction. There's no overturned glass, so if he drank the poison, it didn't hit him immediately. Neither cookie on the floor has any bites taken out of it, so if the poison was in a cookie, he had already eaten the whole thing. There are no other half-eaten foods here that I can see and no bits of food in his mouth. So, he either drank or ate the poison, and it took a while to take effect. We can guess he was looking into his refrigerator when the effect of the poison hit him because it's ajar. He then stumbled out to the sundeck clawing at his throat."

Before anyone could respond, a loud crashing sound came from the bedroom. Rosa and Miguel rushed to the room. On the wooden floor, a drinking glass had broken into several pieces. A little of what appeared to be orange juice was splashed across the hardwood floor. On the top of the dresser sat Diego, calmly staring down at the mess. He then looked up at Rosa with his head slightly cocked to one side and meowed.

"Oh no, Diego!" Rosa cried. She reached for the kitten and picked him up. To Miguel, she said, "I'm so sorry. I completely forgot about him."

Miguel joined Rosa, who now stared at the spilled juice. They looked at each other.

Miguel turned to Officer Richardson who waited in the doorway. "We need photographs, someone to collect this broken glass, and a sample of this liquid for evidence. Also, check to see if there is a pitcher of juice in the fridge."

Officer Richardson perked up at Miguel's instructions. "Yes, sir."

LEAVING the police to search the house further, Rosa and Miguel drove back to the Police station, and Rosa couldn't keep from apologizing about Diego.

"It was very unprofessional of me to let him out of my sight. He contaminated evidence."

"It's possible the glass had already been tipped over," Miguel said. "At any rate, no real damage was done." He gave her a warm sideways glance. "Let's maybe just keep this little tidbit from Delvecchio."

Rosa appreciated the grace he extended to her, and was quite sure none of the other members of his team would've gotten off so easily. It helped that Diego was frightfully adorable.

"Two murders in one week." Miguel blew air out of his pursed lips. "You would think this was south central LA! I'd wager a guess the post mortem will reveal that we have two victims who died from the same poison. There's someone out there with motive who knows them both."

Rosa hummed in agreement. "And we already know there is a connection between the two victims. I saw them together on the beach."

"Exactly." Miguel kept his eyes on the road. "Shirley Philpott remains our prime suspect, but then there's Vanessa Forrester as the possible spurned lover in a love triangle. What possible motive would either of them have to kill Jason Brewster?"

Rosa had the same question. "The one thing that connects them all is the party at the beach—an event organized to raise money for a specific charity."

"Why don't you dig around a bit more on the subject of that CPRF charity? Maybe you can ask your aunt a few more questions. I'll interview Vanessa Forrester."

"Do you think it might be a better idea for me to be the one to talk to Vanessa?" Rosa asked. "In my experience, if a detective is going to interview a lady about a possible affair or love triangle, the truth could be more forthcoming if that detective is a woman."

"Hmm, yes, you're probably right." Miguel pulled the cruiser into the police lot. "Or . . . maybe if *I* took Diego with me to interview the former Mrs. Clarence Forrester, her guard would drop. I mean—" He gifted Rosa with a grin. "—as we have seen already today, women can't resist a kitten."

"Diego isn't ready for police work," Rosa said protectively.

"He's got to earn his badge at some point."

"*Nooo*." She pulled Diego closer to her chest.

"Okay, we'll give him a few days. Then we'll deputize him."

"He's not even house-trained yet!"

"I honestly don't think Detective Sanchez is either, and yet they let him work here."

"Pffft," Rosa said. "C'mon Diego. Let's get you home before Detective Belmonte tries to draft you into public service before you're ready! Besides, it's time to meet your new family."

13

"Oooh, what do you have there?" Gloria squealed.

"His name is Diego." Rosa put him down on the grass in the backyard of the Forrester mansion, and the kitten sniffed the surrounding area. Aunt Louisa and Grandma Sally were lounging by the pool, Aunt Louisa worshiping the sun, and Grandma Sally well-covered in umbrella shade.

Gloria knelt to pet him. "He's so sweet!"

"Do you think you could be a dear and run into town to get some pet supplies?" Rosa asked. "I was on my bike when I found him."

"Sure. But first, I'll get him a dish of milk. He looks pretty hungry." Gloria ran back into the house.

Louisa, her eyebrows furrowed behind her

sunglasses, rose from her chair at the pool and glided over to Rosa. "What on God's green earth is that?"

Rosa had anticipated this kind of reaction from her aunt, but before Rosa could answer, Grandma Sally launched a commentary. "Louisa doesn't like house pets. She lost one as a child and never recovered."

"I wasn't a child, mother. I was nineteen."

"And ready for a husband and children. I told you you'd forget about that cat if you had a baby. And I was right."

Louisa scowled at her mother, then redirected her angst at Rosa. "Don't listen to the meanderings of an old know-it-all."

Grandma Sally's grin grew smug, and Rosa was relieved when Señora Gomez stepped out of the sliding glass door. One thing Rosa knew about her relatives was that they never aired their dirty laundry in front of the staff.

"*Ooh, que lindo gatito!*" She caught Rosa's eye. "Can I hold him?"

Rosa grinned. "Certainly."

Señora Gomez gently lifted Diego off the grass. "Where did you get him?"

"I found him beside the bakery in a discarded box. I think he was abandoned."

Señora Gomez cradled Diego in her arms and

covered him with kisses while he purred loudly. "*Mi pobre pequeño querido*. My poor little darling."

Gloria returned with a dish of milk and put it down on the ground. After Señora Gomez had placed Diego in front of the bowl, the cat hungrily lapped the milk.

Aunt Louisa's frown deepened.

Thankfully, Gloria defused the bomb. "Look Mom, isn't he cute? He must stay with us!"

"I don't remember granting permission for a pet in the house." Aunt Louisa narrowed her eyes and stared pointedly at Rosa while holding a palm out in Grandma Sally's direction. Grandma Sally's mouth had opened to speak, but her daughter's ultimate authority on all things family had caused her to shut it again.

"Yes, well," Rosa started, a sudden feeling of defiance rising in her chest. "There are one or two things that I don't remember giving my okay on recently as well."

"Oh, phooey," Aunt Louisa said with a toss of her bouffant. "You're not still bothered by my chat with the mayor, are you?"

Rosa lifted a brow. The truth? She wasn't upset anymore and was quite enjoying the challenge.

Resignation finally appeared in her aunt's expression, and she tilted her chin toward Diego. "The creature can stay, but you should plan on taking it with you when you go back to England."

"Of course." *Whenever that was*, Rosa thought as it suddenly dawned on her she wasn't in any hurry to book that return ticket. For some reason, England seemed like a receding object in her rearview mirror.

Aunt Louisa turned back to the pool.

"Actually, Aunt Louisa, if you have a few minutes, I'd like to talk to you about your charity work with the Polio Foundation."

"Come join me at the pool," her aunt said.

"I'll take Diego," Gloria offered, then lifted the kitten.

"I'll bring you both some iced tea." Señora Gomez went back inside while Rosa and Aunt Louisa sat at a glass patio table.

Aunt Louisa's lacy pink dress billowed in the breeze. She crossed her legs then tilted her head. "How is your investigation going?"

Rosa jumped right in. "There was another murder this morning."

Aunt Louisa's jaw dropped. "That's a shock."

"The man's name is Jason Brewster. Does that ring a bell?"

Aunt Louisa's gaze moved to the pool as she considered the question, then she shook her head. "No, I don't think I've heard that name. Who is he?"

"He's an accountant in town, but the police also suspect he sold drugs. He was at the fundraiser."

Aunt Louisa tucked her chin. "What? Not as a guest, he wasn't. I knew everyone on the list."

"His house is located up the beach from where the party was, so he could've just been a random person in a public place. The thing is, Aunt Louisa, I saw him arguing with Florence Adams not long before her body was found."

Señora Gomez arrived with two glasses of iced tea. Grateful for the refreshment, Rosa and her aunt both took a sip.

Rosa continued. "Mr. Brewster was also at the scene of the crime, but he walked away when he saw me watching him."

Louisa clicked her tongue. "A drug dealer at my event. As if a murder isn't bad enough."

"Aunt Louisa, did you know much about Florence's personal life? Did she have a boyfriend? Was Jason Brewster her boyfriend?"

"Flo had many boyfriends."

Red spots appeared on Aunt Louisa's cheeks, and Rosa knew she'd hit a sore spot. Clarence had been one of those many boyfriends.

"I'm afraid Flo's reputation in that regard was in tatters," Aunt Louisa said. "If it weren't for her relationship to Shirley, I would have sent her packing."

Rosa waited, knowing that if the silence stretched out too long, Aunt Louisa might fill it. She was rewarded.

"I've already told you about Flo's tendency to drink too much, so I guess I am not totally surprised that she was somehow connected to this drug dealer." She paused for a moment. "Do you think the two murders are connected?"

"It's possible. What was Florence Adams' role in planning the charity event?" Rosa took out her notepad from her purse.

"Mostly, the allocation of funds. We all voted on it, but she had a heavy influence on where the money was spent."

"Such as?"

"Well, there were campaigns to promote and support the new vaccines currently used to combat polio. The hospital in Santa Bonita is always in need of new equipment to treat the disease. In particular, the iron lung machines, although they cost more than they're really worth, so we are not concentrating on those much anymore. There was an expansion of the children's ward last year with more staff and equipment needed for polio rehabilitation."

"I see." Rosa scribbled on her notepad and then looked up, "Who else is on the board?"

"Shirley Philpott, of course. She helps with the

promotion of our events. Then there's Raul Mendez. He takes care of our accounting—"

"How long has he been on the board?" Rosa took another sip of her drink.

"Several years now. He lost a younger brother to polio a few years ago, but that was before I was with the charity. Rod Jeffers is on the board. I think you met him at the event. He's a polio survivor."

"The man with the leg braces?"

Aunt Louisa nodded. "He also helps with promotion of the events and is our liaison and spokesman to the press." Louisa took a final sip of tea and pushed away from the table. "I am afraid I have a meeting this morning. We can talk later if you want."

Rosa smiled with appreciation. "You've been very helpful, thank you."

Aunt Louisa stepped away, paused, and looked over her shoulder. "I just want to say that I am relieved that you are on this case. I know you had reservations."

*T*hough Vanessa Forrester and Rosa had technically been related through marriage, her divorce to Clarence had been finalized, so Rosa felt assured that Vanessa wouldn't feel very cousinly toward her. Having told Miguel that she'd do the interview, she knew she needed to get moving.

Deciding that Gloria's presence would probably put Vanessa at ease and more willing to answer Rosa's questions, Rosa approached her. "Gloria, I need to speak to Vanessa again about the case. Would you like to come along?"

Gloria's eyes brightened. "As part of your investigation? I could take notes. You know, maybe I should become a journalist!"

"We don't want to scare her," Rosa said. "It would be best if you committed the conversation to memory and wrote up notes later." *Having notes to refer to would be a good thing*, Rosa thought. Gloria could come in handy, after all.

Gloria worked her lips. "You're right, of course. It's best if we act natural."

Rosa, delighted with Gloria's enthusiasm, fought back the grin that edged its way to her lips. "Precisely."

LEAVING Diego in Señora Gomez's care, Rosa and Gloria took the Bel Air, with Gloria driving, to the north district of town. Gloria twisted the large knobs on the chrome-plated radio and gaily sang along with "Rock Around the Clock" by Bill Haley and the Comets.

"I love this group, don't you?" Gloria's smile was as bright as a clear summer day. "Their tunes make me want to dance." She swayed her shoulders to emphasize the fact, causing Rosa to laugh out loud.

Gloria parked in front of a modest apartment building on the corner of two quiet streets. Rosa couldn't hold in her surprise. She'd imagined the wife of Clarence Forrester and the granddaughter of Aunt Louisa would live in something more substantial.

"I know what you're thinking," Gloria said, staring back at Rosa. "Mom adamantly insisted that Vanessa live with us despite their marriage problems." Gloria grinned mockingly. "What would people think? It was bad enough that the word 'divorce' was even being mentioned aloud. Vanessa never took Mom's threats seriously, and when she left, the Forrester money was shut off with no option for Vanessa ever to move back. I tried to reason with Vanessa, but she's as stubborn as my mother. Vanessa now manages a shoe store to get by while Julie is in playschool."

When they approached the main door, Gloria pushed a button next to the name Forrester on the outdoor directory.

"Hello?" The voice that came over the intercom seemed slightly out of breath.

Gloria spoke loudly into the intercom. "Vanessa? It's Gloria. I'm here with Rosa."

After a moment, a buzzer sounded, and Gloria pushed the glass entry door open.

They took the elevator to the third floor and gently knocked on Vanessa's door. Dressed in white exercise shorts and a cotton top that tied in a bow at the back of her neck, Vanessa wore her brown hair tied back into a ponytail. With intense brown eyes, she carefully regarded Rosa as she opened the door.

"Pardon how I look. I was just doing some calisthenics in my front room." Vanessa invited them into a small but comfortable-looking apartment. The living room, smelling faintly of cigarette smoke, had a window that offered a beautiful view of the surrounding neighborhood. An exercise mat and some small barbells next to it, lay on the vinyl floor.

Vanessa invited them to sit at a small table situated in a dining area next to the kitchen.

"Can I offer you a drink?" Vanessa said politely. "I have Coca-Cola in the fridge."

Feeling somewhat parched, Rosa accepted the offer. Gloria did the same. Vanessa opened a shoulder-high, single-door fridge, poured the bubbly beverage into three glasses, and carried all three in a triangular shape to the Formica-topped table.

"I'm assuming you're not here for a friendly visit." She pulled up a speckled vinyl-covered chair for herself and nodded at Rosa. "We met briefly at the party the other day. Your accent is definitely not from around here."

"She's my cousin from England," Gloria said proudly.

Rosa sipped her soda pop and set the glass on the table. Condensation ran in rivulets to create a wet ring. "I'm here on holiday."

"Of course, I've heard about you." Vanessa crossed a bare leg. "Clarence says you're a detective?"

"She's a WPC," Gloria answered with a giggle. "That stands for Woman Police Constable."

Vanessa smirked. "Nice of the men to make the distinction."

Rosa ignored the jibe. "I'm part of the London Metropolitan Police Force. I've been asked to join the investigative team in Santa Bonita on the Florence Adams case."

Vanessa narrowed her gaze in Gloria's direction. "How fab."

Rosa cocked her head, "Yes, I guess that's . . . um . . . fab." She pushed a stray strand of her chestnut hair behind her ear. "Do you mind if I ask you a few questions?"

Vanessa pouted. "I was already questioned by Detective Belmonte. I don't know what else I can add."

"I know, but sometimes it's good to go into things a bit deeper after the fact." Rosa jumped in. "How well did you know the victim?" She watched Vanessa's face intently for her reaction.

Vanessa blinked several times. "Not well. We weren't friends or anything like that."

"Vanessa," Gloria broke in gently, "The police know about Clarence and Flo."

A red flush bloomed on Vanessa's cheeks. "It's difficult to keep private matters private in a town this size." She stared at Rosa. "You can see why I'm reluctant to talk about it." She jutted her chin out defiantly. "It's humiliating."

"I understand," Rosa said, and she did. The reason she was in California was to escape the tide of public humiliation that had roared her way after she'd abandoned Winston. "But this is a murder investigation, so, unfortunately, hard questions will be asked. If you hold back any information, and the police find out, it'll immediately cast suspicion on you."

Vanessa swallowed. "I see."

"Based on the statement you gave Detective Belmonte, you were walking along the shore when you came upon the body, correct?"

Vanessa nodded.

"How long had you been on your walk?"

"I guess about twenty minutes."

"Did anyone see you or talk to you at that time?"

"No, I walked south along the shore for a while and then turned around. It was starting to get dark. I . . . don't think anyone saw me. I mean, there were a few people in the distance that weren't part of our group. The beach wasn't crowded, but it wasn't deserted either. They were all strangers to me, though."

Rosa had taken her walk at the same time, only she'd headed north while Vanessa had gone south.

"I'm sorry that I have to get personal here, but how long had your husband and Florence been involved before you found out?"

Vanessa lifted a creamy white shoulder. "A couple

months? Who knows? It's not like Clarence would tell me the truth."

"I'm sorry my brother hurt you," Gloria said.

"Yeah, well. Looks like Florence got the worst of it."

A heavy pause settled between them.

Gloria shifted uncomfortably before breaking the silence. "What are you implying?"

"Oh, nothing. Just fate. Florence was a home-wrecker, and now she's dead."

A smile tickled Vanessa's lips in a way that made Rosa still. Vanessa jumped to her feet and collected the empty glasses. "I don't mean to be rude, but I have to pick Julie up from her friend's house, and I need to make myself presentable before facing the public.

WHEN ROSA and Gloria arrived back at the Forrester mansion, they found Clarence in the garage—*an apparent refuge from a houseful of women*, Rosa thought—working on a motorcycle.

"A new bike?" Rosa asked as she and Gloria leaned against the rounded chrome fender of Aunt Louisa's Ford and admired the gleaming red and white motorbike.

"Yes, just bought it in February. It's a Moto Guzzi Falcon. A beauty! I'm planning a trip down to San

Diego soon. Just giving it a bit of tune-up." Clarence tugged on a spark-plug wrench, then stood up and wiped down the bike with a rag.

"We just came from Vanessa's apartment," Gloria said.

Clarence stopped wiping for a second, but then returned to polishing as he spoke. "Oh?"

Rosa got straight to the point. "Were you and Florence Adams still involved at the time of her death?"

Clarence sighed. "No. What happened between me and Flo happened months ago. It was a stupid mistake and only happened once. A drunken night at a party. Vanessa and I had problems, and Flo was all too willing. Vanessa got really frosted when she found out —I suspect Flo told her—and announced she wanted a divorce."

"It only happened once?" Rosa said, surprised. "Vanessa made it sound like you had an ongoing relationship with Miss Adams."

Clarence's eyes narrowed to angry slits. "Is that what she said? That woman really likes to light up the tilt sign."

Rosa raised her eyebrows and glanced at Gloria for interpretation.

"He means she likes to lie a lot," Gloria said.

Clarence continued his sad tale. "I told Flo we'd

made a mistake, and we needed to go our separate ways, but she wouldn't have it. She badgered me for weeks. I made another big blunder attending a social event with her—after Vanessa and I had split up—but it was more out of an effort to placate her. When I tried to put on the brakes, Flo lost it."

"How do you mean?" Rosa asked.

"She'd follow me around, come over to the house unannounced, phone me incessantly . . . it went on for quite a while."

"That lines up more with my memory of things," Gloria said. "I remember her ringing the doorbell and Bledsoe telling her you weren't available. She had a fit."

"Did this unwanted behavior stop?" Rosa asked.

"She finally gave up, then started hanging on to some other guy's arm. Brewster's the name. Likes to wear Hawaiian shirts."

Clarence's motive for killing Florence Adams dissolved if his story about Miss Adams finding a new crush was true.

But was it? All Rosa knew for sure was the two people in Clarence's story were now dead.

Just then, Señora Gomez entered the garage carrying Diego.

"There you are, Miss Rosa," the housekeeper said as she handed over the kitten.

Rosa scooped Diego into her arms and pressed her

lips to his fuzzy head. "Hello, cutie pie. I hope you were a good boy?"

"El gatito se portó perfectamente," Señora Gomez said with a smile. "I was looking for you, Miss Rosa. You have a message. Detective Belmonte wants you to meet him at the medical examiner's office right away."

15

"It had us baffled for a long time, and we still don't have it all figured out." Dr. Rayburn said, his southern drawl warm and slow as maple syrup. He sat down on one of the chairs in the medical examiner's visiting room along with Melvin Philpott, who sat in another chair, while Miguel and Rosa took a seat on the large leather sofa. "But we're a bit closer. I hope ya don't mind, but I've asked Dr. Philpott to sit in on this meeting. He's not on the investigative team, and he's not examined either of the bodies, but I consider his experience and expertise valuable in any brainstorming sessions we might have."

"Dr. Rayburn has done an excellent job on this," Melvin Philpott said. "Whoever poisoned Florence, and now this Jason Brewster fellow, underestimated the science of pathology. I also believe this will steer the investigation away from my wife."

"I hope so," Miguel said. "But of course, you know we have to keep all options open. Your wife is one of several suspects that have possible motives for the death of Florence Adams."

Dr. Philpott nodded his head begrudgingly.

Miguel addressed the assistant. "What have you discovered, Dr. Rayburn?"

The Texan cleared his throat. "Well, I couldn't really confirm this because such small amounts were found in Miss Adams' blood. But when Mr. Brewster's blood showed the same compounds, I knew we were onto something." He smiled at Rosa, taking his time to continue. "After examinin' the orange juice sample you brought in, we were able to confirm the data enough to make a judgment." He pulled out a sheet of notes from a folder and lay it on the desk. "Remember that I mentioned the death resembled gas poisonin', in particular one derived from Phosgene? Phosgene was developed before World War One for the purpose of makin' certain plastics. However, they then used it in the war as a poison gas after it was discovered that inhalation would cause death."

Dr. Rayburn paused as if to give the seriousness of this revelation time to sink in. "Its military designation became CG. It was harder to detect than chlorine because it was colorless and smelled like freshly cut hay. However, it took a little longer to affect the lungs of the victim than chlorine gas. In the end though, it proved to be more devastatin' because the enemy couldn't necessarily tell when it was deployed."

"And you're saying this particular gas was found in the lungs of our victims?" Rosa asked.

Dr. Rayburn's eyes latched on to Rosa in a way that made her feel admired.

"That's what I'm sayin' ma'am."

"But how?" Miguel asked. "I mean, as far as we can tell, Miss Adams was supposedly standing at the edge of the pier."

"Well, that's just it," Dr. Rayburn continued. "The intriguing question for these two cases is how are you going to administer it in gas form? I'd propose that y'all are looking for a new kind of derivative, a mutant kind of phosgene, if you will, that was produced by using some of the same compounds mixed with certain chemical catalysts and binders to form a drug which can be ground into powder. I won't bore you with all the chemical processes and names but suffice to say, someone has developed a new poison that is tasteless, can be slipped into a drink, and will have an opioid, or deadenin' effect on the medulla oblongata. That part of the brain is mostly responsible for the involuntary function of breathin'.'"

Miguel was aghast. "A poison that tells your brain to stop breathing?"

Rosa shared his dismay. "That's dreadful!"

"From what we can tell, the substance would have a delayed reaction of about thirty to forty-five minutes before being fully absorbed into the bloodstream." Dr. Rayburn stared back solemnly. "Someone slipped it into Miss Adams' drink, a martini according to what we found in the stomach, and when it finally took effect, she died of suffocation. There would have been no warning."

"We assume the same thing happened to Jason Brewster," Melvin Philpott said. "The orange juice sample had a good amount in it."

Miguel leaned over to Rosa, "See, I told you we need to deputize that cat."

Rosa rolled her eyes but couldn't keep from grinning.

Turning back to Dr. Rayburn, Miguel asked, "Have you ever come across the poison before?"

"In a word, no. We can't find any reference to it in our medical books. Our knowledge of exactly how it is made and formed into a powder is simply not there. We have no record of it. That's why it took us so long to piece together what we do know. However, now that we have the orange juice sample, it won't be long before we can more accurately classify it."

"Onvocyn," Rosa said quietly while staring down at the floor. She looked up and noticed everyone staring at her. "It's called Onvocyn."

Melvin Philpott shook his head. "I don't think I have ever heard of that."

Rosa struggled to think of how to explain herself without giving away her source—her mother's personal journal. Her entries during the years of the First World War had been sparse and annoyingly, but understandably, vague, or worse, rubbed out beyond deciphering. Rosa, a frequent visitor to the London Library, had to do considerable searching to find out what Onvocyn was. Most of the time her intense pursuit of trivia proved to be merely an enjoyable waste of time. Once in a while, it came in handy. Like now.

"It's a substance that was developed by the Germans about midway through World War One," she explained, "but it was hard to make and took a long time. One needed exactly the right atmospheric conditions during production, or else it would be contaminated and rendered useless." Rosa stared back at the stunned faces of the three men in the room, then continued. "It was used a few times successfully during espionage operations by the Germans and then later by the British, but was strictly banned by both sides after the war. Unfortunately, it did show up in Britain on the black market. Drug gangs in London have been known to disguise it as cocaine when they wanted to get rid of rivals and make it difficult to determine the cause of death."

"How in the blue blazes of hell do you know all of that?" Melvin Philpott finally exclaimed.

"I . . . I . . . read it in some Scotland Yard case files, I think."

"Who on earth would have access to such a substance, and why use that particular one?" Miguel asked. "There are lots of other poisons that are far easier to obtain."

"The killer obviously put a lot of thought into what kind of results he or she wanted," Dr. Rayburn remarked.

"*Por todos los santos*" Rosa and Miguel both exclaimed out loud simultaneously. They looked at each other in surprise.

"Let's see," Miguel cleared his throat. "It had to be a powder or a pill, and it had to be tasteless when slipped into a drink. It's possible the killer wanted a poison that produced a delayed reaction for some reason."

"Agreed. As for who would have access, that's a tricky one," Dr. Rayburn said. "Substances like this can only be tracked down through the black market."

"Jason Brewster," Rosa said.

The men bobbed their heads in agreement.

"We can now refine our investigation a bit," Rosa offered. "We're looking at someone who had a motive, someone who was at that party, and someone who had a connection to Jason Brewster."

"That certainly points away from my wife, thank goodness!" Melvin Philpott proclaimed. "She certainly had no connection with any blasted drug dealer and has no interest or connection to any secretive, bloody poison used by the Germans over forty years ago!" His voice reverberated and hung in the room.

Rosa looked directly at the older pathologist. "Perhaps, sir. But *you* might."

"You've got some nerve, young lady!" Dr. Philpott ripped off his glasses to reveal wild and angry gray eyes.

"Now calm down, Melvin," Miguel said, putting a palm up. "Miss Reed's only stating the obvious here. As an experienced man of medical science, you know how the criminal element operates in our region. It's not a stretch to imagine that you could have taken on your wife's offence, which gives you motive. You could know about this unheard-of substance and could figure out how to get it."

"I take it you mean I'm interested in the old man's money," Dr. Philpott shot back. "You know as well as anyone, Miguel, that there was no love lost between me and that curmudgeon. If it were up to me, I'd give all that money away should it be passed down to us."

"It's my understanding that it *will* be passed down to you," Rosa said quietly.

"That remains to be seen! Shirley and I are not in agreement about that." Dr. Philpott stared over his glasses at Miguel. "You've known me and my wife for a long time, Mick. I find it inconceivable that you would suspect either of us of murder. And not of one person, but two. It's outrageous!"

Miguel nodded solemnly. "I agree it's outrageous, and I give my word that I will turn over every rock to get to the truth. If you are innocent, which of course, I am inclined to believe, then you have nothing to worry about, do you?"

This seemed to calm Dr. Philpott down somewhat. He gave both Miguel and Rosa a look and then stood. "I have a golf appointment, so if you'll excuse me, I will take my leave."

Silence filled the room after he slammed the door on his way out.

16

It was silent in the police car for the first few moments.

"You stole my saying," Miguel finally said.

"I did not."

"Yes, you did. *Por todos los santos.* That's mine. I inherited it from my grandmother."

"Pfft," Rosa scoffed. "Well then, consider it a tribute to her."

"It sounds funny when you say it, though. Like the Queen ordering a burrito or something." He glanced sideways at her and smirked.

Rosa couldn't help but chuckle. "Thank you, by the way, for defending me back there."

"Don't mention it."

Miguel stopped at a traffic light. "You know, Dr. Philpott is normally a very amiable guy."

"Anyone would react the same way." Rosa palmed her hairdo, reining in any stray strands. "I don't blame him for getting upset."

Miguel signaled to turn, then pulled on the large cream and chrome steering wheel. "I have some matters to attend to at the office, which will probably take a few hours. Delvechio wants me to give a short instruction to a few new recruits on office protocol."

This suited Rosa as she was ready for some time alone. "Would you mind if I spoke to Shirley Philpott again?"

"Wow, you are one brave lady," Miguel said with a glint of admiration in his eyes. "You just royally ticked off the Mister, and now you want to pay a visit to the already highly agitated Missus? Be my guest."

"*Royally?*" Rosa raised her eyebrows and shot him a sidelong glance. "Really, Miguel?"

"Sorry, I forgot you Brits are a kind of possessive of that word."

"No . . . it's fine. I just think you misused the word, that's all." Rosa held in a grin.

"Well, when you see the Queen, which I am sure happens often, give her my apologies. Also, my best to that Duke of Edinburgh guy too. I'm not sure who he is, but he always seems to be lurking around Queen Lizzy for some reason."

Rosa turned her face to the side window to

suppress another grin.

Once in the back lot of the police station, they climbed out of the police cruiser, and despite their recent casual banter, offered polite, if not rather awkward goodbyes. There were moments when it was easy to forget the missing years between them. Rosa had to remember that Miguel was engaged to be married.

One must guard one's heart!

As Rosa pulled away in the Bel Air, she decided to return to the Forrester mansion to talk to Gloria. Her younger cousin had proven invaluable in the last interview, and since this one might get testy, it would be good to have an ally. She would make Gloria promise not to divulge any information from the case to anybody.

To Rosa's surprise, she was almost knocked over when Gloria came racing around the living room corner dragging a little cloth mouse on the end of a string.

"Oh, sorry," Gloria said, laughing and out of breath. She sat down on one of the upholstered armchairs as Diego awkwardly ran around the same corner looking for the mouse. "He's been keeping me busy. He's quite the little predator."

Rosa picked up Diego and nuzzled him to her neck, but after a short cuddle session, the kitten wriggled out of her grasp, landed on the sofa, and scampered away.

"Goodness," Rosa said.

"Not in the mood," Gloria said lightly.

"I'm on my way to interview Shirley Philpott," Rosa announced. "I'm wondering if you could join me?"

"Sure. Señora Gomez won't mind watching Diego. Give me a minute to get ready."

Gloria disappeared up the steps while Rosa located Diego and handed him over to the housekeeper. "I do appreciate you keeping an eye on the little fellow," Rosa said. "Please keep him out of sight of Aunt Louisa and Grandma Sally."

"Si, Miss Rosa," Señora Gomez said. "They don't get along with little Diego."

After what was definitely longer than a minute, Gloria, wearing a stylish cherry-red dress, sashayed into the kitchen where Rosa waited.

"I'm ready!"

THE PHILPOTTS LIVED in a comfortable neighborhood in the south end of Santa Bonita. Their house was a sprawling, single-story ranch-style home with a two-car garage and beautifully manicured front lawn. Shirley Philpott, her salt-and-pepper hair framing her round face, welcomed Rosa and Gloria with a tentative smile. Once her guests settled around the kitchen table, she poured lemonade out of a large carafe into two glasses and handed them to Gloria and Rosa.

After a short time of polite conversation, Rosa got to the point. "Do you know a man by the name of Jason Brewster?"

Mrs. Philpott blinked coldly. "Now, there's a question that the police did not ask."

Gloria hesitated, looked into her glass, then glanced at Rosa.

"Oh, for Pete's sake," Mrs. Philpott exclaimed. "I didn't poison your drink! Would you like me to drink first?" She poured some into her own glass and took a large gulp. After patting her lips with a tissue, she answered the question. "I believe someone by the name of Brewster assisted Florence in. . . certain unsavory ways."

"Cocaine?" Rosa ventured.

Mrs. Philpot sniffed. "Yes. If you must be so on the nose about it."

"Your husband says that you are not in agreement when it comes to the disbursement of the inheritance money you're due to receive from your uncle," Rosa said. "Is that true?"

"It is. We have enough money; that is not the issue. The truth is, I plan to donate most of it; a lot of it right here to our own polio charity. Melvin doesn't even want it on our personal books. He can be quite stubborn sometimes. There's not a good history between him and my uncle, as you obviously know by now. My husband's being unreasonable. By law, the money will have to show up on our books."

Rosa couldn't ignore her growing thirst and dared to drink her lemonade. "Can you elaborate more on your history with the polio charity?" she asked after a sip.

Shirley crossed her legs and sighed. "Let me see, where should I begin?"

"When did you join the organization?" Rosa asked.

"Oh, I think it was now over five years ago. I was on the board long before your Aunt Louisa got involved. Melvin and I had both supported various polio foundations over the years, but when we found this one, right here in Santa Bonita, we focused a lot more of our efforts here close to home." She glanced between Rosa and Gloria with somber eyes. "I lost an uncle to the horrible disease."

"I'm sorry," Rosa said. Globally, polio was a devastating disease. Any advancement made by science was welcomed. "Aunt Louisa says you were involved in promoting the charity?"

"Yes, I work a lot with Rod Jeffers. I think you met him at the party. He's the man with the leg braces."

Rosa remembered the man casually looking on from a patch of lawn while Miguel and Melvin Philpott examined the body on the beach. "He helps me relate to the press for any events we are doing," She took another sip of her drink.

"What kind of connection did Mr. Jeffers have to Florence?" Rosa asked.

Mrs. Philpott pursed her lips. "Within any organization, there can be tensions among the members. Rod is amiable enough, albeit a bit shy sometimes, which is odd for someone who works with the press, I know. But Florence, well, she could be a bit testy, and that's certainly not a secret. What was secret though, was the fact that she had a heart condition. Not everyone knew that. She was being treated for it."

Mrs. Philpott's gaze drifted to the palm trees out the window, their fronds blowing lightly in the wind. "She told me it was in control, but I found myself constantly watching her for signs of a heart attack or something, especially because she was so irritable at times. I was always the one trying to calm her down when the stress got too much. Earlier, on the evening she died, she was terribly upset. She had overheard somebody talk about her. I tried to calm her down, but she'd had a few drinks so . . ." Mrs. Philpott sighed. "But now, from what the police and Melvin have told me, it wasn't her heart that got her, it was poison."

Gloria looked into her glass again. Shirley shook her head and chuckled somewhat ruefully.

"Goodness, child. How long have you known me?"

Gloria straightened up and finally took a sip. "How long has Rod Jeffers had those braces on his legs?"

"I'm not sure. I think since he was very young. He seems to get on quite well, and his condition is not as bad as many others we've seen."

"Do you have other polio survivors on the team?" Rosa asked.

"Not at the moment. Did you know that the latest statistics show that polio is in decline?" Mrs. Philpott's demeanor brightened. "They say it's largely due to breakthroughs in vaccine therapy and the programs for mass vaccinations. There's still no cure for someone who already has the disease, as you know, although I've heard that in some cases, it can still lessen the symptoms if the subject is young enough."

"Yes, I've heard that too," Rosa replied. "It's good news. Organizations like yours have had a lot to do with the decline in polio cases."

Mrs. Philpott smiled. "Yes. It's gratifying."

Rosa inclined her head. "What did you mean by 'at the moment'? Did you, at one point, have someone else on the team who was a polio victim besides Rod Jeffers?"

"No, not really. But Raul Mendez had a cousin,

Juan Mendez, who died last year from issues related to polio. Raul and Juan were fairly close. Rod Jeffers also knew Juan well."

"Exactly how did Juan Mendez die?" Rosa asked.

"His lungs gave out, or more specifically, his diaphragm and the involuntary muscles that control breathing stopped working. If it's left unchecked, the disease eventually paralyzes those muscles and death comes by asphyxiation."

A hunch that something important had just been disclosed hit Rosa, and she felt a faint buzzing of her nerves. "And there's no way to prevent that from happening?"

"Well . . . yes, there is," Mrs. Philpott answered. "A polio victim can be kept alive with an iron lung, a machine that supports muscles necessary for breathing."

"Was an iron lung not available for Juan Mendez?"

"All the machines in the Greater Los Angeles Area were being used at the time. They're very expensive and take a long time to show up after being ordered. One iron lung machine could cost the same as a small house."

"So," Rosa began, "even though your charity focuses on raising money for polio, you couldn't get a machine for a relative of one of your own members?"

"We never really found out if we could've

managed to raise the money. Time ran out on us. The subject had been debated ad nauseam at our board meetings, mind you, but polio is in such rapid decline nationally that, it was argued, we should focus our efforts on other, more inexpensive initiatives." Mrs. Philpott shook her head. "I don't know if any of us realized the full extent of the immediacy of Juan Mendez's situation. Anyways, by the time the motion was passed to focus on an iron lung for Juan, he'd passed away. It was rather sudden."

Rosa's heart beat just a little faster, and she leaned forward on her chair. "Who were the ones on the board that were most reluctant to buy a machine?"

Shirley Philpott sat back in her chair. "At first the board was in favor of the purchase, but it was Flo who campaigned against it. In the end, the vote was split down the middle. Florence was the swing vote. She voted no. I remember now, that both Raul Mendez and Rod tried desperately to sway her, but she was unmovable."

"Mrs. Philpott," Rosa began, "why did you avoid me downtown when I called out to you? I know you saw me."

Red patches bloomed on Shirly Philpott's round cheeks. "I was embarrassed. I knew everyone thought that I'd killed my cousin."

hrough his open office door, Rosa could see Miguel sitting at his desk—the receiver of his black telephone cradled between his shoulder and his ear. Not wanting to intrude, Rosa waited for the phone call to end. She didn't mean to eavesdrop, but how could she avoid hearing the conversation?

"I can't come to L.A. right now, Charlene. I'm in the middle of a case."

Charlene? Oh, dear. Miguel was talking to his girl-friend. Rosa's chest tightened, and her stomach dropped.

Even though Rosa stepped back into the hallway, Miguel's voice drifted. "I thought you were coming here? No, I know you're busy too. Look, I have to go. I'll call you later, and we can compare calendars. Okay. Miss you too. Bye."

Rosa took a long, slow breath and pushed her shoulders back. She was a professional. She was here out of duty, not for a social call. She tapped purposefully on Miguel's door then stepped in.

The scowl etched on Miguel's face smoothed into a smile when he saw her. "Oh, good, you're here."

Rosa didn't waste time on pleasantries. "I think we need to focus our attention on Rod Jeffers, and possibly, Raul Mendez." She sat down in the chair opposite his desk.

"Um . . . okay, and hello to you too."

Rosa blushed. "I'm sorry, hello."

Miguel's dark eyes flashed with amusement then grew serious. "You do realize that Raul is in my band and was onstage the night Florence was killed. He has an excellent alibi."

"I know. I haven't figured that part out yet."

"You also realize that Rod Jeffers is a cripple. Although possible, it would have been hard for him to catch up with the somewhat frenetic movements of Florence Adams the night of the murder *and* surreptitiously slip something in her drink. No one that I've interviewed so far even saw him having a conversation with her that night."

Rosa folded her gloved hands in her lap. "Then we have to figure that out too."

"You also realize," Miguel continued without being

condescending, "that as far as we know, neither of those two people have any connection to Jason Brewster or anything to do with abstruse poisons."

"As far as we know." Rosa held up a gloved finger in the air. Her mind worked hard to bring all the parts together. It was almost like eating a piece of that black taffy so popular in California; it required some thoughtful chewing.

"Yes, as far as we know. We . . ." Miguel stopped and just looked curiously at Rosa with her finger still pointing, frozen in midair. "Okay, sure, here's the part of the conversation where we can have a pause." He shrugged his shoulders. "And believe me, I am a big believer in dramatic pauses. But, when you're ready—I mean, we don't want to rush it of course—you tell me some of the information that I don't already possess."

"Both Raul Mendez and Rod Jeffers have motive," Rosa said finally. "In fact, they have the *same* one."

Miguel sat expectantly, waiting for her to elaborate.

"Well, don't just sit there," Rosa said, bounding to her feet. "It's time to grab the keys from your wall again. The game's afoot!"

"Really, Rosa? *The game's afoot?*"

"It's what Sherlock Holmes always says when he is closing in on the quarry!" Rosa impatiently waved her arms at him.

He rose from his chair and grabbed the car keys from the wall.

"Okay, I'll drive, you talk," Miguel said as they made their way to the back door of the station and out to the parking lot. "You'll let me know if I should put the siren on, right? I like that part."

"Not just yet." Rosa climbed into the passenger seat and gave Miguel the details of the interview with Shirley Philpott. "She knows both men and their connection to the poor lad who died waiting for an iron lung."

"I didn't know any of that." Miguel shook his head. "I mean, I knew Raul had a younger cousin who died from polio, but I had no idea about the part played by the charity, specifically our first victim."

"Shirley Philpott never felt right to me as the prime suspect in this case," Rosa remarked.

"Me, neither," Miguel admitted. "It was hard for me to imagine her killing anyone or anything, much less committing two murders, but I had to follow the evidence."

This Rosa understood.

After stopping at Rod Jeffers' apartment but getting no answer at the door, they questioned the landlady, a woman in a full apron with dull brown hair covered by a scarf tied at the back of her slender neck.

"Mr. Jeffers is usually at that fitness gym in town

this time of day," she said, leaning on a broom. "He takes a taxi since he can't drive on his own with those bum legs."

Miguel knew the place and parked on Lear Street in the business district of the town in front of a building with a sign that read *Jimmy Gym's Fitness Club*.

"Clever name," Rosa said.

They were greeted by the sound of Chuck Berry's "*Maybelline*" blasting over the loudspeakers. Though the room was filled with various fitness equipment, the room was empty at this time of day, with the exception of Rod Jeffers, who was prone on a bench with his crutches lying on the floor beside a gym bag.

Miguel walked over to the desk. "We just need a minute with our friend over there." The young man looked up from his magazine just long enough to nod and went back to reading.

At first, Mr. Jeffers didn't notice them. He adjusted his leg braces and, using his arm crutches for support, brought himself to a standing position. Except for his legs, which looked rather emaciated, he seemed to be fit with well-defined arms and chest. He obviously liked to keep himself strong despite his illness.

Rosa and Miguel caught up to Mr. Jeffers just as he reached the door to the men's changing room.

Miguel called out, "Rod?"

Rod Jeffers' eyebrows collapsed into a *V*. "Miguel?"

"Yes. Sorry to interrupt your workout."

Mr. Jeffers glanced at Rosa with a look of disdain and sniffed.

Miguel jumped to an introduction. "This is Detective Rosa Reed from London's Metropolitan Police. I believe you met at the event where Miss Adams died?"

Rosa held out her gloved hand. "Hello, Mr. Jeffers."

Rod Jeffers hesitated then leaned an arm crutch against his body, shook her hand, then re-engaged the crutch before it toppled to the floor. Rosa had to admire his agility, even though she felt terrible that she'd thoughtlessly made him perform it.

Mr. Jeffers turned to Miguel. "What's up?"

"We are hoping to have a few words with you if you don't mind."

Mr. Jeffers looked surprised. "Oh . . . sure . . . but . . . I have to use the restroom first." He pointed with one of his crutches to the men's room door.

"That's fine," Miguel said. "We can wait."

After Mr. Jeffers had disappeared into the restroom, Rosa grabbed Miguel's arm and nodded towards the gym bag Mr. Jeffers had left on the floor.

"I can't just look through that," Miguel said quietly. "That's against police protocol."

"Good thing I'm not a member of *your* police force," Rosa said slyly. "Go and distract the man at the desk for a minute."

"We can't let Rod know we looked in his bag." Miguel narrowed his eyes at her then turned towards the reception desk which, thankfully, was partially hidden from view.

Rosa rushed to look inside the bag. Inside were two towels, some toiletries, and a large bottle of pills. The word *Dihydroboldenone* was written on the label. Rosa quickly took out her note pad and wrote the word down. She then closed the bag and walked over to Miguel just as Rod Jeffers came out of the men's room. Together, they walked into the lounge area and sat down. Miguel closed the door, and the boom of the rock and roll lessened to a level more conducive to conversation.

"Looks like you keep in pretty good shape," Miguel said.

Rod Jeffers smiled with a cocky grin. "Thanks, it's pretty much necessary for me to keep my upper body strength. It helps me in terms of walking and stuff."

"I've heard that athletes or people who are serious about conditioning their body sometimes use steroids," Rosa said casually.

Miguel shot her a questioning look. Rosa continued, unfazed. "Apparently, they are quite helpful when one wants to build muscle mass."

Mr. Jeffers didn't blink. "I'm just interested in staying strong enough to drag these legs around."

"Certainly, I'm not suggesting that someone like you would use steroids." Rose smiled, hoping to disarm the man. "I understand they're rather hard to get hold of."

"Yeah, so?" Rod Jeffers glared back then focused on Miguel. "What gives, Miguel?"

"Just humor the lady, my friend."

Rosa's chest warmed at Miguel's show of trust.

"If one were interested in obtaining steroids, Mr. Jeffers, do you know how one would go about it?"

"Well, ma'am, *I* for one, wouldn't know," he said snidely. "Now, tell me why you're askin'?"

"Rod, your manners," Miguel chastised.

"I don't get why she's asking me questions."

"I didn't get a chance to interview you the other night at the beach," Miguel said

"Yeah, well, wasn't feeling great, so I took a taxi home." His eyes darted from Miguel to Rosa and back. "Is that what this is about? The fact that I left the beach before you could talk to me? Miguel? We're friends. You can talk to me anytime. No need to ambush."

"We didn't mean to offend," Miguel said, "but I'm

afraid I have to take this matter seriously. Florence Adams was murdered."

The muscles around Rod Jeffers' mouth twitched. "*What?* I thought she fell off the pier."

"The evidence proves otherwise," Miguel said. "There was also another murder in Santa Bonita just yesterday. Does the name Jason Brewster mean anything to you?"

This time Mr. Jeffers did blink. Twice. "No, I don't think so. Do you think he's the killer?"

"Where were you two nights ago between the hours of six p.m. and three a.m.," Miguel pressed, ignoring Rod's question. The time represented the estimated time of death of Jason Brewster that Dr. Rayburn had provided.

"I was at home, of course. I don't really get out that much, as you can understand."

"Were you with anyone?" Rosa asked.

Rod Jeffers met her gaze with reluctance. "Raul and I were playing crib on my back patio. We do every Monday night."

"Just you and Raul? No one else?" Miguel asked.

"Yes, and nope."

Miguel and Rosa looked at each other.

"Tell us about Juan Mendez," Rosa said.

Rod Jeffers raised his eyebrows, shook his head,

and looked sincerely surprised. "What's he got to do with anything?"

"We don't know yet," Rosa said. "Perhaps you can tell us."

Mr. Jeffers scowled at Rosa. "I don't know what I can tell you, Mick, that you don't already know. I mean, you must have heard about Juan." Staring at Miguel, he added, "He was Raul's cousin."

"I've only known Raul since he joined my band," Miguel said. "About a year. I'd heard he had a cousin who died from polio, but I didn't know the whole story."

Rod Jeffers leaned back in his chair and crossed his arms. "I'm not sure what you mean by the 'whole story'."

"You and he were quite close, weren't you?" Rosa asked.

"Juan and I grew up together in Mansfield. We were the same age," Rod Jeffers replied.

Rosa remembered that Mansfield was a small town just north of Santa Bonita.

"Isn't that where Raul grew up as well?" Miguel had now taken out his notepad and started writing.

"We all went to elementary school there. Raul is two years older than Juan and me."

"When did polio enter the picture?" Rosa asked.

Rod Jeffers sighed deeply. "Juan got it first when

we were both in sixth grade. At first, everyone thought it was just a bad case of the flu. I contracted it about five months later. In those days, there was no vaccine."

Rosa concurred. Field tests of the first vaccine didn't happen until 1954.

"Juan's illness progressed differently from yours, I assume?" Rosa said.

Rod Jeffers slowly nodded. "His lungs got paralyzed."

Miguel tapped his pen on the table. "From what I understand, an iron lung could have prolonged his life?"

Mr. Jeffers answered darkly. "It could've *saved* his life."

"But there was none available," Rosa said. "Is that right?"

Rod Jeffers hesitated. "Apparently not."

"From what we heard," Rosa said gently, "the charity foundation tried to get him one, but it was expensive. By the time they decided to place an order, Juan was dead."

Rod Jeffers shifted in his seat, grimacing. "Something like that, yes."

"Was Florence Adams in on that decision-making process?" Miguel asked.

"I didn't kill her," Rod Jeffers said forcefully.

"We didn't say that you did," Miguel returned.

"But you're obviously thinking it. Look, I was furious with Florence Adams—enraged beyond words. She stalled and stalled while my friend slowly suffocated to death! I bet you anything that if he hadn't been from south of the border, those funds would have come much faster."

His bitterness was a heavy weight in the room. Rosa inexplicably found it challenging to breathe.

"I hated Flo Adams for what she did," Mr. Jeffers said. "I held her responsible for the death of my friend. I never forgave her. There's your motive if that's what you're looking for, so go grab your handcuffs and take me away if it makes you think your job is done. But the real killer, whoever he is, would still be at large." He narrowed his eyes on Miguel. "I swear on my mother's grave, I didn't kill her."

18

*M*iguel pulled the police cruiser away from the curb in front of Jimmy's Gym. "What do you think?"

Rosa removed her compact lipstick with its attached mirror, turned her back to Miguel, and covertly applied some before facing him again. "I can't quite decide if I believe him about not murdering Florence Adams. I mean he's pretty convincing but . . ."

"I agree. He's a hard guy to read."

"He *is* lying about the steroids, though."

"Oh?"

"Yes. I wrote down the name on the pills I found in his bag." Rosa retrieved her notepad from her purse. "I'll have to check with Dr. Rayburn to confirm, but as far as I know, *Dihydroboldenone* is a steroid used by bodybuilders and the like. From what I've read, it's kind of a new fad in the world of athletics. If that's true, then Mr. Jeffers is lying."

"*Dihydroboldenone* isn't illegal," Miguel said. "So, the only reason I can think he'd lie would be about how he got them."

"Or from whom?"

Miguel's eyes registered understanding. "Jason Brewster."

"Exactly," Rosa said. "It's possible that Jason Brewster supplied Rod Jeffers with steroids. I noticed Mr. Jeffers appeared to be physically fit when I first saw him that night on the beach."

Miguel nodded. "That makes sense. I'd just read the report from Detective Sanchez when you arrived at my office today. They found steroids in Jason Brewster's bathroom. A rare kind—apparently, you need a connection to the black market for it. Now the post-mortem didn't find any in his blood, so he may or may not have been using them. But if Jeffers is lying, it means he didn't want us to know that he had any connection to Jason Brewster."

"Precisely. Did the police find anything else there?"

"No, not much. They're still going through some articles, but nothing really stands out."

"Hmm, perhaps something will still turn up," Rosa

said. She hoped evidence that connected either Rod Jeffers or Raul Mendez to Jason Brewster would be found.

"Well . . . there is one thing come to think of it," Miguel said.

Rosa glanced sideways over her sunglasses. "What's that?"

"From what we can tell, Jason Brewster wasn't a smoker. There was no telltale odor in the house or any ashtrays, and Dr. Rayburn's autopsy report confirmed it. However, on the back sundeck, someone had taken a bowl from a matching set they found in the kitchen and used it as an ashtray. A single cigarette butt was found on an outdoor table along with ashes in a bowl. If the ashes had been there for a couple of days, they would have either been blown away by the slightest breeze or been soaked from that rain we had the night before. The ashes were dry."

"That means the cigarette was probably smoked the evening before." Rosa tapped her lips with a fingernail.

"Correct."

"And our killer is a smoker."

"Very likely."

"I can't imagine Rod Jeffers smoking," Rosa said.

Miguel turned onto the main street of the town. "A

guy with polio whose best friend died of asphyxiation? I should think not."

"Wait, what kind of brand was the cigarette?" Rosa asked.

"It was a weird Mexican brand of menthols." He grinned at Rosa. "I hang out with a lot of Mexicans. It took our guys a whole day to track down the brand, *Delicados.*"

Her mind jumped to Raul Mendez at the Legion and their awkward yet informative encounter.

"That's the brand Raul Mendez smokes!"

Miguel hit the steering wheel with his palm. "You're right. I've seen him smoke menthols at rehearsals. They smell terrible."

Rosa and Miguel stared at each other as the implications resounded. Miguel's friend could be involved.

"I need to get back to the station," Miguel said, his brow etched in dismay. "On the way, I'll stop to pick up the bass guitar from our rehearsal space downtown."

"Why?"

"Raul's fingerprints will be all over it. If we can match it to the fingerprints on the cigarette butt—"

"Of course," Rosa said. *A match of fingerprints would be strong evidence.*

"I'll get Sanchez to expedite the lab. He can be quite pushy when he wants to be."

"Good thinking." Rosa tapped the toe of her black flats. "In the meantime, I can interview Rod Jeffers' neighbors. Hopefully, someone had witnessed Raul Mendez on Monday night for that crib game."

ROSA LEFT Miguel at the station and drove the Bel Air to Rod Jeffers' home. Large drops of rain began to fall, and Rosa fumbled around to find the wipers. Just as she pulled up to the apartment building, it started to pour. Rain this heavy was likely a rare occurrence this time of year for California. She reached for the umbrella she'd stowed in the back seat of the car—a habit from her life in England—then hurried to the covered entrance.

Next door to Mr. Jeffers lived Mrs. Benson, a middle-aged widow who talked about Rod Jeffers in glowing terms. "He's always friendly, and has a good attitude considering his condition."

When Rosa questioned her about the regular crib nights, she replied, 'Yes, that Mr. Mendez fellow comes every Monday night at seven, and they play in the back yard. He parks his little red car right in front of the building. Honestly, I don't know how that thing keeps running, it's a real rattletrap. You can hear it clunking as he comes around the block."

Rosa had the feeling that watching the neighbors was a regular pastime for this lady.

"Can you hear them while they play?"

The game itself wasn't loud, but players certainly could be if there was enough passion for the competition.

Mrs. Benson frowned. "I can, but I don't eavesdrop, mind you."

"No, of course not. But isn't it annoying to you? I mean, having that go on every Monday night?"

"They often get quite excited and start talking pretty loud. I don't mind though. I'm just glad Mr. Jeffers can have an enjoyable night with his friend."

"Can you make out what they're saying?"

"Only when they talk loud like that, even then it's hard to understand every word." She grinned. "It's not like I lean against the fence."

Rosa grinned back and wondered if the kind neighbor had just told her a little white lie. "Did they play last Monday night, Mrs. Benson?"

"No. But Mr. Mendez came back later that night around midnight, which is very unusual, and it woke me, which *did* annoy me a little."

"How did you know it was Mr. Mendez?"

"I recognized the clunking of his old car."

Rosa pursed her lips in response. Mr. Mendez had

probably come by to let Rod Jeffers know the deed was done.

RETURNING TO THE POLICE STATION, Rosa parked and stepped out with umbrella in hand. The rain had stopped, but dark clouds on the horizon continued to threaten. Rosa found Miguel in his office in an in-depth discussion with another plainclothes officer.

"Ah, here she is. Rosa, I want you to meet Detective Bill Sanchez. Bill, this is Miss Reed, known in London as WPC Reed. She's agreed to consult with us on this case."

Detective Sanchez looked to be in his mid-thirties with unruly, dark hair, dark eyes, and a brown complexion like Miguel's. His rumpled white shirt and crooked red tie looked like he'd slept in them. He had a half-smoked cigarette hanging out of his mouth, but Rosa thought it looked unlit.

"WP—*what?*"

"WPC Reed," Rosa said, extending her hand. "Woman Police Constable with Scotland Yard."

"Well, imagine that!" Detective Sanchez stretched out his hand, "Miguel speaks highly of you." He winked at Miguel. "You didn't tell me she was a 'looker,' amigo."

Miguel blushed, and Rosa shared his embarrassment.

Miguel cast a sheepish glance her way. "You'll have to excuse this guy. He wasn't raised with some of the *finer* sensitivities the way that I was." Miguel slapped Detective Sanchez on the arm. "Officially, he's my partner here at the precinct, but I think of him more as my mascot—fun at a ball game, but—"

"Very funny," Detective Sanchez cut in. His cigarette remained gripped with the part of his mouth that wasn't grinning.

"Anyway," Miguel continued, "Sanchez is going to take the bass guitar over to the lab, and hopefully, we can get the results back quickly. If we have a match with both the cigarette stub and the guitar, and maybe even from some of those shards from the glass that your cat tipped over, that would be compelling evidence."

"You had a *cat* at a crime scene?" Detective Sanchez's forehead buckled dramatically. "Is that how they do it in Scotland?"

"Sanchez, she's English, not Scottish," Miguel said. "Can't you tell from her . . . wait . . . is that an umbrella?"

Both Sanchez and Miguel looked down at the black umbrella Rosa had with her and then shared an amused look.

"Yes, I know it's very British, but it *is* raining out,

you know," Rosa said defensively. "Any good Londoner always has one of these about." She shook it at them both scattering drops of water onto the floor.

"Point taken," Miguel chuckled.

"You were thinking of Scotland Yard, Detective Sanchez," Rosa said turning to Miguel's partner. "A common misconception."

Detective Sanchez appeared sincerely stumped. "Why's it called Scotland Yard if it's not in Scotland?"

"Because the original building of the London Metropolitan Police was on a street called Great Scotland Yard.

"In Scotland."

"In London," Rosa corrected."

Detective Sanchez opened his mouth and lifted a finger in the air as if to make a point, but then just dropped his hand and shook his head.

"To answer your question," Rosa said, returning to the detective's original query. "We don't normally have cats on the job in London, but in this case, I had a kitten with me, but . . . it's a long story."

Detective Sanchez tipped his hat at Rosa. "I'll head to the lab and get back to you both when I learn something."

"So, what did you find out from Jeffers' neighbor?" Miguel asked, once Detective Sanchez had left.

"Her name is Mrs. Benson. My suspicion was

correct. Mr. Mendez wasn't there on Monday night. Mr. Jeffers lied about that. But he did come late in the night for some reason. Mrs. Benson is quite certain about that."

"Time to go talk to Raul," Miguel said, reaching for his keys. He turned to Rosa, "Let's go, I know where he lives."

ROSA STOOD to Miguel's side as he rang the front doorbell of Raul Mendez's tiny house on the edge of town, receiving no answer. Dejected, they returned to the unmarked car. A young man who was busy pulling a plastic rain tarp over a motorcycle called out to them.

"You just missed him. Left about ten minutes ago!"

"Do you know where he went?" Rosa called back.

"Train station. I was putting the garbage bins out when he walked out of his front door with a suitcase. He got into a cab. I heard him tell the driver to take him to the main station."

Rosa felt a thread of excitement vibrate down her spine. "Rod Jeffers must have called him! He probably guessed that we're onto him."

Miguel hurried to the driver's side of the car. "He's bolting."

Rosa jumped in just as Miguel gunned the engine.

"This is so hard to believe." Miguel pulled out the

flashing light and placed it on top of the roof. "I've been playing gigs with that guy for almost a year!" He hit the switch for the siren, then accelerated.

"Which way do you think he'd go?" Rosa shouted over the wailing of the siren.

"There's a route on the Pacific Surfliner," Miguel shouted back. "It heads to San Diego Union station. From there, it's effortless to catch a bus to Tijuana. I know Raul still has family in Mexico. If he makes it there—"

"Rod Jeffers' neighbor called Mr. Mendez's car a 'rattletrap'." That must be why he's taking the train."

"Faster too." Miguel kept his eyes squarely on the road in front of him. "I think there's a train that goes straight to San Diego once a day. I used to take it all the time to go visit relatives in Rosarito."

"Do you know what time?"

"Five forty-five, I think."

Rosa checked her watch. "It's five-thirty."

Unfortunately, the rain began in earnest, and the roads were slick with water. Miguel was forced to slow down. He expertly guided the cruiser around traffic as cars stopped in deference to the police siren.

When they approached the vicinity of the station, Miguel cut the siren and the lights to avoid alerting Raul Mendez to the fact they'd arrived. As they jumped out of the car, Miguel said, "You go around the other way. If he sees one of us, he might run."

The Santa Bonita train station was not a large building, certainly not the kind of station Rosa was used to using in the vast network of underground and overground lines in London. Instead, it was a modest two-story, *Spanish-Revival-style* construction with red clay roof tiles and a terra-cotta stucco exterior. It had two main entrances, one at either end of the building.

Rosa hurried into the south entrance while Miguel went into the north. She scanned the entries to the shops and saw there was a short queue at the ticket counter. Mr. Mendez probably already had his ticket and was out on the platform. Rosa glanced at the large clock on the wall: five forty-three. They had only moments.

Without an arrest warrant, Rosa wasn't sure if the police had the authority to stop a train just to question someone. She rushed out onto the crowded south-bound platform and looked both ways. About fifty people waited to board the train and stood in groups at each train car's entry door. Rosa slowly worked her way north in search of the familiar figure of Raul Mendez. Far down, at the other end, she spotted Miguel as he made his way towards her. But Mendez was nowhere to be seen. Could he have already gotten on the train?

As the last of the people boarded, the loud voice of a ticket agent yelled, *"All aboard!"*

Just then, about sixty feet to her left, Raul Mendez emerged from one of the doors marked *Men's Restroom.* Rosa watched him look to his left. *Did he see Miguel who was three car lengths away?*

Miguel had not yet noticed him, but when Raul saw Miguel, he started jogging in Rosa's direction. She then realized she was between him and the nearest car entry door. Raul hadn't spotted her, so she slipped behind a broad support post that held an extensive arrival schedule. Just as Raul sped by, she stepped out from behind the post, and with the wooden, curved handle of her umbrella, hooked his ankle, sending him sprawling to the pavement.

Rosa stood over him, the sharp end of the umbrella pointing at his throat. *"En garde!"*

19

"It looks like Raul is ready to confess," Miguel said into the phone. "Can you come down to the precinct? As one of the lead investigators, I thought you'd like to be here."

"I'll come right now."

The day before, when they had arrested Raul Mendez and brought him to the precinct, he had been belligerent and refused to speak until his lawyer was in the room. Rosa knew from experience that if a first-time killer was going to confess, it was often after a night in jail and a phone call to a lawyer.

Rosa quickly changed into a striped sea-foam-green and pink dress, which matched her pink flats. She arranged for Señora Gomez to keep an eye on Diego, collected the keys to the Bel Air, and headed for the garage.

When she entered the precinct, Rosa couldn't help but notice how Miguel's eyes flickered as they moved up her figure to her face, then met her gaze. It was a brief acknowledgement of attraction, but he quickly looked away, inhaled, and took on an expression of professionalism.

"Raul's lawyer just arrived," he said, getting straight to business. "Raul requested representation as soon as I told him we'd collected his prints from a cigarette found at the home of Jason Brewster. He, of course, had denied even knowing Mr. Brewster." Miguel continued with his update as they headed to the interrogation room. "I'm pretty sure that convinced him that a full confession would serve him better than a 'not guilty' plea."

Miguel placed a hand on the doorknob in front of them. "I guess I'll be looking for a new bass player. We also picked up Rod Jeffers right after we got Raul. He's confessed to his part in the murder—giving Raul a false alibi.

They entered the room, which was sparsely furnished with a table and four chairs. A reel-to-reel tape recorder was set up on the table along with a small microphone. Rosa sat down just as a middle-aged man, wearing a black business suit and carrying a briefcase, walked in, followed by Raul Mendez. The man intro-duced himself as John Fellows, acting legal counsel for

Raul Mendez. Raul's face looked impassive as he took a seat beside the lawyer and opposite Rosa and Miguel.

"Let's get right to it," Miguel said as he pushed the record button on the tape machine. He then stated the time and date and the names and occupations of everyone in the room, saying Rosa Reed was a *Special Investigative Consultant* by order of the Mayor's office and the Chief of Police.

"Why did you kill Florence Adams?" Miguel asked.

Raul sniffed heavily. "She was responsible for the cruel and unnecessary death of my cousin Juan Mendez. She held his life in her hands and stonewalled the board of directors at the polio foundation repeatedly. You better believe that if Juan was white and his name was John, she'd have voted to fund the iron lung on the first day.

"Instead, she stalled until—" His voice constricted with emotion, first with grief, then malice. "It was the worst kind of betrayal. I wanted her to suffer. I wanted her to feel what Juan felt. Choking to death, clawing at his chest just to get a breath of air. Juan didn't deserve to die, especially not like that."

"How did you get the poison in her drink?" Miguel asked.

"I knew that we had the song '*Autumn Leaves*' on our set list." Raul looked at Miguel, who stared back

Murder at High Tide

questioningly. "There's no bass on that song, you play it on your own on the guitar."

Miguel nodded his head in realization, "Of course."

"That gave me time to leave the stage while giving me somewhat of an alibi since the poison had a delayed reaction. No one would point me out as talking to the victim right before she started choking. It was an easy thing to offer Florence a drink from the open bar." He scoffed. "Her glass always emptied fast."

"How did you get her onto the end of the pier?" Rosa asked.

"That was not part of the plan. I wanted her to start choking in plain view of everyone as a testament to what happened to Juan. I knew the martini would spill onto the sand and make it irretrievable for the police should they suspect poison. By the way, I have to compliment your pathology team; apparently, it's almost impossible to detect Onvocyn in the blood-stream, much less know what it is."

Miguel glanced at Rosa and offered a subtle congratulatory smile.

"In any case," Raul continued, "Florence got in some argument, and when I got back onto the stage, I saw her wander out onto the pier. It was about twenty-five minutes after she'd drunk the poison, so I suspected she would die out there—possibly even falling into the ocean, which would make the cause of death even harder to discern."

"How was Rod Jeffers involved in all of this?" Miguel asked.

"He wasn't, really. He *was* very close to Juan, they were good friends, and I did confide in him early on. He was in favor of killing Flo, at first, but as we got closer to the evening, he chickened out. I told him as long as he kept his mouth shut, he didn't have to help me in any way."

"That still makes him an accessory," Rosa interjected. "He also tried to cover for you by giving you an alibi the night of the Brewster murder."

Mr. Mendez shrugged. "Yeah, I suppose."

"Why did you then kill Jason Brewster?" Miguel asked, leaning slightly towards the microphone.

Mr. Mendez palmed his shirt pocket subconsciously as if looking for a phantom pack of cigarettes, then let his hands fall to his lap. "That was regrettable, but he threatened to go to the police, even though I told him that was stupid and would implicate him. Brewster had quite a thing for Florence, you know. I didn't know this when I contacted him. He also didn't know that she was the reason I wanted the poison."

"So, you slipped it into his drink," Rosa said.

Mr. Mendez snorted again. "I went over to try to calm him down, talk some sense into him, ya know, but he was a mess. I couldn't risk him ratting me out, ya know? It was easy to slip the same poison into his orange juice when he wasn't looking.

"How did you know about Onvocyn?" Miguel asked. "That's a scarce drug."

"It took me a long time to find it; long hours at the Los Angeles Public Library studying poisonous substances. I wanted one that would bring about the desired effect with about a half-hour delay.

"I knew Jason Brewster was supplying cocaine to Flo and had some connections to the black market. He supplied a lot of drugs to others here in the area, although I wouldn't know who. Even with his considerable connections, it took months for him to get just a few capsules of the stuff and it cost me over a thousand dollars, but in the end, it worked."

The room went silent, the last sentence hanging ominously in the air.

20

*I*n bare feet and dressed in high-waisted, print shorts and a white T-shirt, twisted into a knot at her belly, Rosa ran down the long hallway of the Forrester Mansion. She headed toward the large study which had formerly served as Uncle Harold's personal office and library when he was still alive. She dragged a long string with the little cloth mouse dangling on the end.

Giggling like a schoolgirl and slightly out of breath, Rosa collapsed on the leather sofa and peered back down the hallway. Diego had slowed down and lowered to a crouch with his belly an inch from the carpet, his tail thick and fluffy as if he had suffered from an electric shock. His eyes were intently focused on the toy mouse as he slowly crept down the hall towards the stuffed creature. Rosa pulled the string slightly to make the mouse wiggle. Diego froze for a moment, and then crept forward again. Rosa put a hand to her mouth to stifle another giggle.

Suddenly the kitten jumped high in the air and landed on the mouse. He grabbed it with his forepaws and lay on his side as he bit and kicked it with his back claws.

"Diego!" Rosa lost hold of the string but watched him proudly. "Aren't you the little hunter?" Diego stopped chewing on the mouse, looked up at Rosa, and coughed. He rose shakily to his feet and after a few more deep coughs, vomited up a hairball onto the expensive Oriental rug.

"Oh no!" Rosa jumped to her feet. "Not on the carpet." She scooped up Diego and stared down at the small gray wad on the rug. *Ugh*, she thought. *I'd better clean this up before—*

"Rosa!"

Rosa cringed at the sound of her aunt's voice.

"What on earth has that animal done to my Chobi Oriental?" Aunt Louisa, with her hands braced on pointy hips, glared with narrowed eyes. "That rug was imported from India!"

"I'm so sorry, Aunt Louisa, I'll have it cleaned for you right away."

Before her aunt could continue with her scolding—or worse, ban Diego from the house—Bledsoe, thankfully, appeared in the doorway. "Excuse me, ma'am, but a Detective Belmonte is on the telephone for Miss Reed."

Rosa knew her aunt was loathe to put on any display of familial disunity in front of the staff and used that to her advantage to scurry out of the room with Diego under one arm and the toy mouse in the other hand.

She whispered to her cat as she walked down the hall, "Vomiting on a lady's carpet is not a way to her heart, Diego."

The kitten, utterly unfazed by the event, purred softly in her arms.

"Hello, Detective Belmonte," Rosa said as she pressed the receiver to her ear. Her pulse picked up at the mere idea that she would hear Miguel's voice across the line.

"Hiya, Rosa. I just want to thank you again, officially, on behalf of the Santa Bonita Police Department for your assistance on this case. I quite honestly don't think we could've done it without you."

Rosa blushed at the praise. "I'm certain that's not true," she returned politely, "but thank you for saying so."

"I'm out a bass player, so I guess finding another one is next on my agenda. What about yours?"

That was a loaded question, and Rosa was surprised that Miguel even asked it. He must be as curious about her and she was about him.

"I'm not sure," Rosa answered truthfully. "I need a bit more time to work that out."

"Well, all the best to you. Maybe I'll see you around."

Now that this case was solved, Rosa saw no reason for their paths to cross again.

"Yes, maybe."

GLORIA WAS LOUNGING by the pool when Rosa held up a magazine with a lovely photograph of Audrey Hepburn on the cover.

"Isn't she just so glamorous?" Gloria lowered her sunglasses and stared over the rims at Rosa. "She reminds me of you, actually. You both have striking eyebrows."

Rosa blinked, not sure what to make of what was surely meant as a compliment. "Thank you?"

"Why couldn't I look like her? She's deliciously sophisticated."

"You have a very appealing look, Gloria," Rosa said. "But it's the inside that counts in the end."

"Oh, boo. That's what attractive people say about the plain."

Rosa blew a loud raspberry at her cousin before settling into the lounge beside her. Diego curled into a ball on her lap and purred.

Gloria stared forlornly. "Grandma Sally says it's a waste of good effort for me to go to acting school."

Rosa gave her cousin a stern look. "Gloria, if you want to go to acting school and become an actress, then that's what you should do. No one can stop you, except yourself."

Gloria pushed her sunglasses along the ridge of her nose. "You don't know what it's like to live with two powerful Hartigan women."

Rosa laughed. "Actually, I do."

"Oh, right. High school. I forgot. But your prison sentence was only a few years. Mine's been my whole life."

"I repeat, Gloria. If you want to do something, do it."

"You're right, Rosa, thank you." Gloria's pale, slender legs lifted off the side of the lounger. "I'm going to make a call to the college right now and register."

Rosa smirked as she stroked the top of Diego's head. Aunt Louisa and Grandma Sally wouldn't appreciate her interfering in Gloria's life, but what did it matter now? Rosa would probably go home in a couple of weeks anyway.

The thought left her feeling bittersweet. She missed her family, but somehow, returning to London made her feel like she was going backward.

And then there was Miguel.

"No, Diego, there's no Miguel. He belongs to Charlotte. Or was it Clarice?"

Rosa lifted Diego and pressed her face into his furry body. She knew Miguel's girlfriend's name was Charlene. Charlene Winters. And one day, Rosa would turn on the telly and see Miss Winters' beautiful face on the screen.

Because Miguel's girlfriend would be beautiful.

"That's enough of that, Diego," she said hoarsely. "I've got my own problems to figure out, but not right now, right? I'm on holiday."

Rosa must have dozed off in the shade of the patio umbrella because no sooner had Gloria left, than she'd returned, dressed in striped capri pants and a blue fine-knit top.

"I've done it, Rosa!" Gloria's cheeks were rosy with excitement. "But it doesn't start until September, so boo. But still, lots of fun left of summer. You know the fair came to town today?"

Rosa was having a hard time keeping up with Gloria's wide-awake exuberance. "No, I wasn't aware."

"Oh, it's a lot of fun, with rides and clowns and cotton candy."

None of those things sounded fun to Rosa.

"I don't know—"

Gloria grabbed Rosa's hand and tugged playfully. "Oh, come on. You can't sit around here all day, and I'm bored. Please, come to the boardwalk with me."

A grin tugged on the edges of Rosa's lips. Gloria's energy and zest for life were hard to resist. And her cousin was right. She couldn't very well spend the rest of her holiday sitting around the Forrester mansion. Besides, what could go wrong at the boardwalk?

If you enjoyed reading *Murder at High Tide* please help others enjoy it too.

Recommend it: Help others find the book by recommending it to friends, readers' groups, discussion boards and by **suggesting it to your local library.**

Review it: Please tell other readers why you liked this book by reviewing it on Amazon or Goodreads.

EAGER TO READ the next book in the Rosa Reed Mystery series?

Don't miss MURDER ON THE BOARDWALK.

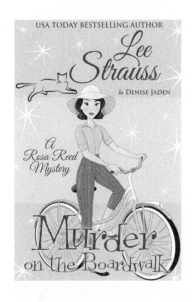

Murder's such a shock!

When Rosa Reed—aka WPC Reed of the Metropolitan Police—and her cousin Gloria decide to spend a fun-filled afternoon in 1956 at the fair on the boardwalk in Santa Bonita, California, they're in for a shocking surprise. After a ride assistant's death by electrocution is determined to be murder, Rosa finds herself entangled once again with her high school sweetheart, Detective Miguel Belmonte. Should she catch the next flight to London before she becomes the next victim?

Buy on AMAZON or read for free with Kindle Unlimited!

FOLLOW DIEGO ON INSTAGRAM!

Did you read the PREQUEL?

Rosa & Miguel's Wartime Romance is a BONUS short story exclusively for Lee's newsletter subscribers.

How it All Began. . .

Like many British children during World War Two, Rosa Reed's parents, Ginger and Basil Reed, made the heart-wrenching decision to send their child to a foreign land and out of harm's way. Fortunately, Ginger's half-sister Louisa and her family, now settled in the quaint coastal town of Santa Bonita, California, were pleased to take her in.

By the spring of 1945, Rosa Reed had almost made it through American High School unscathed, until the American army decided to station a base there. Until she met the handsome Private Miguel Belmonte and fell in love. . .

READ FREE!

AFTERWORD

Invented "science" is a common ploy in all kinds of fictitious works including books, film and television.

In Murder at High Tide, the drug *Dihydrobolde-none* is an actual substance while *Onvocyn* is a creation of the authors' imaginations.

ROSA & MIGUEL'S WARTIME ROMANCE

Rosa Reed first laid eyes on Miguel Belmonte on the fourteenth day of February in 1945. She was a senior attending a high school dance, and he a soldier who played in the band.

She'd been dancing with her date, Tom Hawkins, a short, stalky boy with pink skin and an outbreak of acne, but her gaze continued to latch onto the bronze-skinned singer, with dark crew-cut hair, looking very dapper in a black suit.

In a life-changing moment, their eyes locked. Despite the fact that she stared at the singer over the shoulder of her date, she couldn't help the bolt of electricity that shot through her, and when the singer smiled—and those dimples appeared—heavens, her knees almost gave out!

"Rosa?"

Tom's worried voice brought her back to reality. "Are you okay? You went a little limp there. Do you feel faint? It is mighty hot in here." Tom released Rosa's hand to tug at his tie. "Do you want to get some air?"

Rosa felt a surge of alarm. Invitations to step outside the gymnasium were often euphemisms to get fresh.

In desperation she searched for her best friend Nancy Davidson—her best *American* friend, that was. Vivien Eveleigh claimed the position of *best* friend back in London, and Rosa missed her. Nancy made for a sufficient substitute. A pretty girl with honey-blond hair, Nancy, fortunately, was no longer dancing, and was sitting alone.

"I think I'll visit the ladies, Tom, if you don't mind."

He looked momentarily put out, then shrugged. "Suit yourself." He joined a group of lads—boys—at the punch table, and joined in with their raucous laughter. Rosa didn't want to know what they were joking about, or at whose expense.

Nancy understood Rosa's plight as she wasn't entirely pleased with her fellow either. "If only you and I could dance with each other."

"One can't very well go to a dance without a date, though," Rosa said.

Nancy laughed. "*One* can't."

Rosa rolled her eyes. Even after four years of living in America, her Englishness still manifested when she was distracted.

And tonight's distraction was the attractive lead singer in the band, and shockingly, he seemed to have sought her face out too.

Nancy had seen the exchange and gave Rosa a firm nudge. "No way, José. I know he's cute, but he's from the wrong side of the tracks. Your aunt would have a conniption."

Nancy wasn't wrong about that. Aunt Louisa had very high standards, as one who was lady of Forrester mansion, might.

"I'm only looking!"

Nancy harrumphed. "As long as it stays that way."

Continue reading >>>

Rosa & Miguel's Wartime Romance is a BONUS short story exclusively for Lee's newsletter subscribers.

Subscribe Now!

MURDER ON THE BOARDWALK
SNEAK PEEK
CHAPTER ONE

Lines of gently swaying palm trees and stucco Spanish mansions were set against a cloudless blue sky, and Miss Rosa Reed, known in rainy London, England as WPC Reed of the Metropolitan Police, thought the endless sunshine would never get old. She strolled away from the Forrester mansion in Santa Bonita, California, with her cousin Gloria at her side.

"We need to find you a fuller crinoline," Gloria said, playfully nudging Rosa with an elbow as they neared one of the Forrester vehicles, a two-tone yellow Chevrolet Bel Air parked in the driveway.

Not once in her life in London had Rosa been criticized for her wardrobe. With a mother who owned one of London's highbrow Regent Street dress shops, Rosa had grown up under the influence of stylish and quality fashion, the kind that certainly turned heads in the United Kingdom. Apparently, the California coast was a different story as Rosa had been encouraged more than once to wear something a little brighter, a little tighter, or today, a little fuller.

Then again, those suggestions had come from Gloria and might have said more about Rosa's spirited cousin than they did about California fashions. Already, Rosa regretted giving in to Gloria's pleas to accompany her to the fair recently set up at the board-walk. Rosa preferred the quiet of her bedroom—hers at the Forrester mansion felt as cozy and comfortable as her room at Hartigan House in South Kensington—and a good book. Rosa had a stack resting on her night table, from mystery fiction to the latest in forensic science developments. She'd raided the Forrester mansion library shortly after she'd arrived in Santa Bonita, and had tipped one of the maids to make a run to the local library for her (not daring to go there herself for reasons she'd rather not think of at this time). The gentle purring and warm companionship of her kitten, Diego, was all the socializing Rosa desired, and with a deep breath she had to brace herself for the cacophony sure to come.

Not wanting to face Gloria's wrath if she changed her mind, Rosa was determined to be a good sport.

Gloria looked adorable and rather youthful—seven years Rosa's junior, Rosa often felt ancient at twenty-eight in Gloria's presence—in her pink flared skirt with an embroidery of a sizable French poodle and flat black-and-white leather saddleback shoes.

Gloria stood with one hand on one tiny hip and the other stretched out, palm open. "Keys?"

"Why?"

"You've driven it *all* week. Besides, you have Diego to concern yourself with."

Rosa peeked into her tapestry handbag, or *satchel*, as she liked to call it, where her kitten slept soundly. She'd chosen the satchel more for the comfort of Diego, a brown tabby kitten Rosa had recently rescued, than she had for how it complimented her sky-blue swing dress—the one without a large enough crinoline, apparently—and matching Juliette cap.

Diego had an adventurous personality and didn't, for the most part, cause Rosa any concern when she took him along. A rather fortuitous discovery, since Aunt Louisa had insisted that Rosa keep the kitten with her and not leave "that scraggly thing" behind unless either Gloria or the Forrester housekeeper, Señora Gomez, was available to watch him.

Rosa suppressed her strong feelings of apprehension as she handed over the coveted keys. "Drive carefully!" With an exaggerated shudder, she added, "The way you command a car reminds me of my mum."

"Oh, I love Aunt Ginger!" Gloria smirked at Rosa before snatching the keys. "I don't suppose you'd like to trade mothers?" She laughed before Rosa could come up with a suitable quip and hopped into the driver's side of the Bel Air. In moments, the large engine rumbled to life.

"Why Do Fools Fall in Love" played on the radio, and Rosa mused at how à propos it was for her, the fool who fell in love with Miguel Belmonte, her former American flame and, as fate would have it, who was no longer single.

Gloria, looking away from the road more often than Rosa would have liked, announced, "I'm sure we'll see people I know at the boardwalk. In fact, you might run into some of your friends from high school."

Though born and raised in London, Rosa had spent her high school years in Santa Bonita. Her parents had felt an urgent need to get her out of harm's way during the Second World War, and Rosa suspected some of that angst was due to their involvement with the British secret service, though she could never get them to admit to it to her.

The highway wound along the coast. As Gloria chattered on about the funfair at the boardwalk, Rosa gazed at the gleaming sun. The ball of fire hung over the beach, and blue water rushed to the shore. The scene looked like a postcard picture. In the distance, she saw the Santa Bonita Pier. Bright red bars lined a giant Ferris wheel at the edge of the water.

Almost missing the exit, Gloria stomped on the brake and spun onto the ramp to guide them off the highway just in time.

"Gloria!" Rosa pressed a hand on the Bel Air's sleek crocus-yellow dashboard. "For crying out loud!"

"Oh, chili-pop, honey." Gloria glided around a bend that momentarily hid the ocean, then continued along a curvy road that led them down a steep decline. Rosa didn't relax until they were level with the water.

Gloria managed to squeeze into a parking spot without scratching the paint. Rosa could only imagine how Clarence, Gloria's older brother, took to the odd scuffs sure to appear on the Forrester vehicles.

Rosa reached for her satchel. Diego was awake and no worse for wear.

"Hi, sweetie," Rosa cooed and reached in to pat him. "You've already had your first fair ride, poor thing."

Gloria pretended offense, blowing loudly through lips thick with tangerine-colored lipstick. She led the way to the back of the gravel parking lot and down a short dirt path. Then, quite suddenly, the trail opened to more bright colors and tiny lights than Rosa had ever seen in one place. It was as though Christmas had come early and had exploded across the pier.

"It's stunning!" Rosa said, stopping. Now that they were closer, she could see not only the brightly lit Ferris wheel set against the brilliant blue sky, but also several carnival game tents, a ride with spinning cars, and even a roller coaster! The salty air she'd become accustomed to in the last two weeks took on a new aroma with smells of buttered popcorn and warm sugar.

"It is, isn't it?" Gloria grasped Rosa's hand and pulled her toward the lights and the action.

"You'll have to show me how it's all done," Rosa said while gazing around in awe. She slid her new Riviera sunglasses up onto her forehead to get a clearer view.

They walked onto the base of the pier, and only then could Rosa see most of the exciting ocean-side fair. A large platform sat inland and seemed to hold most of the amusement rides, including the giant roller coaster that made Rosa's stomach turn upside down just watching it. The Ferris wheel turned its slow and steady circulations at the farthest end of the pier. Along the boardwalk and pier, numerous game tents were busy with customers and "carnies" yelling, "Step right up! Be our next winner!"

As Rosa and Gloria meandered down the pier, the dings and clanks and shouts from the carnival games were soon drowned out by lively upbeat swing music.

"Is there a band here?" Rosa asked.

Gloria answered glibly, "Mick and the Beat Boys are playing tonight. They're often here on weekends. Isn't that neat?"

Rosa's pulse jumped at the mention of the band's name. The "Mick" in question was the nickname of Detective Miguel Belmonte. She groaned inwardly. So much for keeping her distance from the man.

Very few people knew of the short but intense romance she and Miguel Belmonte had shared eleven years ago. *Eleven years.* The four months they'd spent falling in love was just a blip now on Rosa's timeline. Ancient history. But despite her best efforts, her body still reacted to the mention of his name.

"There's an amphitheater just ahead, with a dance floor." As Gloria led the way, a gaggle of ladies that Gloria recognized joined them. She called out hello and waved, and the gaggle moved toward them. Turning to Rosa, she added, "See, I told you we'd know people here."

We seemed like the wrong pronoun, but as Gloria leaned in to shake hands and cheek-kiss several women, recognition dawned. A few *were* familiar to Rosa, and one was *particularly* familiar.

A lack of teachers during Rosa's high school years in Santa Bonita had combined students of all ages in large classrooms. More times than Rosa could count, they had turned out the school lights and blacked out windows when an oil field was bombed, or a firebomb was discovered somewhere within California.

"You remember Marjorie, right?" Gloria said, motioning to a pretty girl in a green A-line dress with a black-and-white polka-dotted under layer. She wore her bright-red hair in a long ponytail.

"Rosa Reed!" Marjorie said with a glint in her eye. "It's so nice to see you." She sprang forward to give Rosa a hug, which momentarily surprised Rosa. This very non-English custom of hugging at every hello and goodbye took some getting used to.

"Hello!" Rosa said. Marjorie Davidson had trans-formed from a girl to a woman in the eleven years Rosa had been gone. "You're all grown up!"

Rosa recognized Joyce Kilbourne, and Pauline Van Peridon before Gloria could announce them.

"Hello, ladies," Rosa said. They both wore less flashy dresses, Joyce, a slender brunette in violet and Pauline with a boyish-figure, in navy. If anyone needed a fuller crinoline, it was Pauline.

"Hi, Rosa."

Pauline's voice was soft and gentle. Rosa remembered how Pauline had suffered from shyness as a child.

"Hi, Pauline. So, nice to see you again."

Pauline covered her mouth when she said, "I forgot all about your accent!"

"I'd argue that you're the ones with the accent," Rosa said warmly.

Joyce grasped both of Rosa's hands, leaned in, and kissed her on the cheek. "Oh, Rosa! It's been too long."

To the brunette who had only just stepped into the group behind Marjorie, Gloria said, "And you must remember Nancy."

Rosa's emotions were in a state of disorder as she stared at the young lady with honey-blond hair who gaped back. Older now, Nancy Davidson—now Kline —had her hair styled shorter, and a little more weight rested on her hips and face, but her round blue eyes and cute ski-jump nose were unmistakable.

"Hello, Nancy," Rosa said, stepping closer.

Nancy had been Rosa's American best friend during her days in Santa Bonita through the war years. Practically attached at the hip, they'd done homework together, discovered fashion and boys together, and ultimately, Nancy was the only one to know about Rosa's forbidden affair with Miguel Belmonte.

The girls had continued to write after Rosa

returned to London, but like with Miguel, the effort became too difficult over time. Because Nancy had invited Rosa to her wedding, Rosa had felt compelled to ask Nancy to hers. She had not expected Nancy would come. Or reply, for that matter, and she hadn't.

Without smiling, Nancy said, "I heard you were back in town."

Whether Gloria's impulse to pull the other girls away was an act of sensitivity or merely a need to move things along, Rosa was thankful for a moment to speak with Nancy alone.

"I've been meaning to look you up."

"Uh-huh."

"I ran into your mother the other day at the bakery. She said you've been busy. Three boys?"

"Yes, Eddie Jr., Johnny, and Mikey, ages ten, eight, and six." Nancy risked a smile. "A right handful. Mom's a champ about taking them occasionally so I can forget I'm an old married woman and pretend to be Marjorie's age again."

Rosa returned the smile. "It's why I like hanging out with Gloria."

"Are you here on your honeymoon?" Nancy's eyes darted about in search of Rosa's phantom spouse.

Rosa frowned. "I didn't go through with the wedding." Rosa had done a horrible thing to Lord Winston Eveleigh and walked, rather *ran*, out of St.

George's Church before saying *I do.* "It's a good thing you didn't come."

Nancy's eyes brightened, and Rosa saw a glimpse of her old friend in them. "Golly! Now that sounds like a story I'd like to hear!"

On AMAZON

ABOUT THE AUTHORS

Lee Strauss is a USA TODAY bestselling author of The Ginger Gold Mysteries series, The Higgins & Hawke Mystery series, The Rosa Reed Mystery series (cozy historical mysteries), A Nursery Rhyme Mystery series (mystery suspense), The Perception series (young adult dystopian), The Light & Love series (sweet romance), The Clockwise Collection (YA time travel romance), and young adult historical fiction with over a million books read. She has titles published in German, Spanish and Korean, and a growing audio library.

When Lee's not writing or reading she likes to cycle, hike, and watch the ocean. She loves to drink caffè lattes and red wines in exotic places, and eat dark chocolate anywhere.

Norm Strauss is a singer-songwriter and performing artist who's seen the stage of The Voice of Germany. Short story writing is a new passion he shares with his wife Lee Strauss.

For more info on books by Lee Strauss and her social media links, visit leestraussbooks.com. To make sure you don't miss the next new release, be sure to sign up for her readers' list!

Did you know you can follow your favourite authors on Bookbub? If you subscribe to Bookbub — (and if you don't, why don't you? - They'll send you daily emails alerting you to sales and new releases on just the kind of books you like to read!) — follow me to make sure you don't miss the next Ginger Gold Mystery!

www.leestraussbooks.com
leestraussbooks@gmail.com

MORE FROM LEE STRAUSS

On AMAZON

THE ROSA REED MYSTERIES

(1950s cozy historical)

Murder at High Tide

Murder on the Boardwalk

Murder at the Bomb Shelter

Murder on Location

Murder and Rock 'n' Roll

Murder at the Races

Murder at the Dude Ranch

GINGER GOLD MYSTERY SERIES (cozy 1920s historical)

Cozy. Charming. Filled with Bright Young Things. This Jazz Age murder mystery will entertain and delight you with its 1920s flair and pizzazz!

Murder on the SS Rosa

Murder at Hartigan House

Murder at Bray Manor

Murder at Feathers & Flair

Murder at the Mortuary

Murder at Kensington Gardens

Murder at St. George's Church

The Wedding of Ginger & Basil

Murder Aboard the Flying Scotsman

Murder at the Boat Club

Murder on Eaton Square

Murder by Plum Pudding

Murder on Fleet Street

Murder at Brighton Beach

Murder in Hyde Park

Murder at the Royal Albert Hall

Murder in Belgravia

LADY GOLD INVESTIGATES (Ginger Gold companion short stories)

Volume 1

Volume 2

Volume 3

Volume 4

HIGGINS & HAWKE MYSTERY SERIES (cozy 1930s historical)

The 1930s meets Rizzoli & Isles in this friendship depression era cozy mystery series.

Death at the Tavern

Death on the Tower

Death on Hanover

A NURSERY RHYME MYSTERY SERIES(mystery/sci fi)

Marlow finds himself teamed up with intelligent and savvy Sage Farrell, a girl so far out of his league he feels blinded in her presence - literally - damned glasses! Together they work to find the identity of @gingerbreadman. Can they stop the killer before he strikes again?

Gingerbread Man

Life Is but a Dream

Hickory Dickory Dock

Twinkle Little Star

THE PERCEPTION TRILOGY (YA dystopian mystery)

Zoe Vanderveen is a GAP—a genetically altered person. She lives in the security of a walled city on prime water-front property alongside other equally beautiful people with extended life spans. Her brother Liam is missing. Noah Brody, a boy on the outside, is the only one who can help ∼ but can she trust him?

Perception

Volition

Contrition

LIGHT & LOVE (sweet romance)

Set in the dazzling charm of Europe, follow Katja, Gabriella, Eva, Anna and Belle as they find strength, hope and love.

Sing me a Love Song

Your Love is Sweet

In Light of Us

Lying in Starlight

PLAYING WITH MATCHES (WW2 history/romance)

A sobering but hopeful journey about how one young German boy copes with the war and propaganda. Based on true events.

A Piece of Blue String (companion short story)

THE CLOCKWISE COLLECTION (YA time travel romance)

Casey Donovan has issues: hair, height and uncontrollable trips to the 19th century! And now this ~ she's accidentally taken Nate Mackenzie, the cutest boy in the school, back in time. Awkward.

Clockwise

Clockwiser

Like Clockwork

Counter Clockwise

Clockwork Crazy

Clocked (companion novella)

<u>Standalones</u>

Seaweed

Love, Tink

ACKNOWLEDGMENTS

Many thanks to my editors Angelika Offenwanger, Robbi Bryant, and Heather Belleguelle! I couldn't do this without you guys!

My gratitude extends to my co-writer and overall partner in life and crime, Norm Strauss. Not only for helping me jump start this series with plotting, and jotting first drafts, but for joining me on this adventure called life. I *really* couldn't do it without you.

Made in the USA
Monee, IL
21 January 2021

58267011R00135